No Girls Allowed

Young Heroes of History

By
Alan N. Kay

10668938

WHITE MANE KIDS
SHIPPENSBURG, PENNSYLVANIA

This White Mane Books publication
was printed by
Beidel Printing House, Inc.
63 West Burd Street
Shippensburg, PA 17257-0708 USA

The acid-free paper used in this book meets the guidelines for permanence and durability of the Committee on Production Guidelines for Book Longevity of the Council on Library Resources.

For a complete list of available publications
please write
White Mane Books
Division of White Mane Publishing Company, Inc.
P.O. Box 708
Shippensburg, PA 17257-0708 USA

Library of Congress Cataloging-in-Publication Data

Kay, Alan N., 1965-
    No girls allowed / by Alan N. Kay.
        p. cm. -- (Young heroes of history ; #5)
        Summary: In 1862, determined to participate in the continuing Civil War, two young girls, one, a member of an aid society that helps the wounded and the other, disguised as a boy, a soldier in the Union army, find themselves working together at the battle of Antietam.
        Includes bibliographical references (p.).
        ISBN 1-57249-324-0 (acid-free paper)
        1. Antietam, Battle of, Md., 1862--Juvenile fiction. [1. Antietam, Battle of, Md., 1862--Fiction. 2. Sex role--Fiction. 3. United States--History--Civil War, 1861-1865--Fiction.] I. Title.

PZ7.K178Nm 2003
[Fic]--dc21

                                                                    2003052522

For Rachel and Jaime

Contents

List of Characters vii

Preface ix

Introduction x

Chapter 1 Twins 1

Chapter 2 Decisions 12

Chapter 3 The Ladies Aid Society 23

Chapter 4 Something Better 32

Chapter 5 To the Front 39

Chapter 6 Clara Barton 48

Chapter 7 The Wagon Ride 56

Chapter 8 Tears 62

Chapter 9 Something in Common 68

Chapter 10 The Front Lines 73

Chapter 11 The Next Day 86

Chapter 12 The Soldier 92

Chapter 13 Confidantes 99

Chapter 14 Brothers and Sisters 106

Chapter 15 The Bath 115

Chapter 16 The Visitor 125

Chapter 17 Which Way to Go? 134

Epilogue 139

Preview of Book Six 141

Bibliography 146

Characters

Lynn Rhodes—A 16-year-old girl living with her grand-mother on a lake near Augusta, Maine

Daniel Rhodes—Lynn's twin brother

Mary Adams—A 14-year-old Irish girl living with her uncle's family in the countryside near Philadelphia, Pennsylvania

Thomas Adams—Mary's younger brother who becomes a soldier

Characters based on soldiers in the Union or Confederate army

Clara Barton—A clerk in the U.S. Patent Office who raises money and supplies to bring to the Union army

Cornelius Welles—A missionary and Baptist minister who helps Clara Barton

Major Thomas W. Hyde—Regimental commander of the 7th Maine (Union)

General George B. McClellan—overall commander of the Army of the Potomac (Union)

General Robert E. Lee—overall commander of the Army of Northern Virginia (Confederacy)

Vocabulary words to know

secession—when a state declares that it no longer wants to be part of the United States

Confederacy—the name the Southern states gave to their new country because of the kind of government it had

regiment—a group of 1,000 men organized into an Army unit. Most regiments were formed by local townspeople and politicians.

Preface

What is Historical Fiction and who are the *Young Heroes of History?*

Young Heroes of History focuses on children and young adults who were heroes in their time. Although they may not have achieved fame or fortune, they made a difference in the lives of those near to them. Many were strong in body and spirit, but others managed to do the best they could in the time and place in which they lived.

Although the heroes of this series are fictional, these young Americans are placed in situations that were very real. The events of the time period as well as many of the people in these stories are accurately based on the historical records. Sometimes the language and actions of the people may be hard to understand or may seem inappropriate, but this was a different time.

Introduction

It was a man's war. Men had started it. Men would fight it. Men would end it. At least that is what everyone thought.

Mary Adams and Lynn Rhodes are two very different girls. Mary lives on a farm outside Philadelphia, Pennsylvania, and is from an educated Boston family. Lynn lives in Maine with her grandmother and spends the days playing with her twin brother. The only thing the two girls have in common is that they both do not want to stand by and watch while their brothers do all the fighting.

With Civil War destroying the country in 1861, Mary and Lynn decide to help even if they aren't wanted. Mary joins an aid society and helps to heal the wounded. Lynn disguises herself as a boy and fights alongside the men and boys of the army. Each of them faces different challenges as they struggle to be treated as equals. During the Battle of Antietam, these two very different girls, who chose two very different paths, find themselves forced to work together to not only save the United States of America but to somehow take a stand for women in a war that was only for men.

Chapter 1

Twins

"Last one in does all the chores!" Lynn shouted as she tore off her clothes and ran towards the water. In front of her was a huge lake surrounded by beautiful, tall pine trees. Their needles covered hundreds of branches, creating a thick green blanket that almost completely hid the few houses on the shore. The deep, dark water was fresh and cool, fed by the mountain streams and melting snows.

"Wait, wait!" her twin brother, Daniel, called as he stumbled through the woods. His foot was caught in his pants and he couldn't run and take them off at the same time.

"No way!" Lynn shouted back. She was completely undressed except for her underwear.

"Yaahh!" Daniel screamed suddenly, rushing towards his sister. He would have probably beat her if Lynn wasn't so quick. She turned, took one step onto a nearby log and made a perfect dive.

"Beat ya!" she called as she rose to the surface and took a breath.

"That's 'cuz you cheated," Daniel argued. He was treading water next to her and looking around nervously.

1

"No I didn't," Lynn replied.

"You let me put away the rakes and shovels," Daniel said. He continued to look around the lake to see if anyone was watching them. It was secluded, but if anyone caught a boy and a girl swimming together in their underwear, they would never live it down, especially in a small town.

"That's because I took them out," Lynn answered. She looked around the woods as well. "Would you stop doing that?"

"Doing what?" Daniel wondered innocently.

"Looking all over the place," Lynn replied.

"What if someone sees us?" Daniel asked.

"No one will see us," Lynn said firmly.

"Yeah, but what if someone does?" Daniel asked again.

"Then we'll tell them that it was your idea," Lynn said with a smile as she began to swim away.

"Lynn!" Daniel shouted, splashing her in the face and smiling as well. Lynn splashed back and the two of them quickly started splashing and laughing.

"Look at that," Fred whispered from his spot in the bushes. "They're out there swimming again."

"Yeah," his friend Louie agreed. "Kinda sick, isn't it?"

"What is?" Ralph asked innocently.

"They are brother and sister!" Fred exclaimed, as if that explained everything. "They can't go swimming together in their underwear."

"Oh," Ralph said simply. He frowned a little as he thought about what Fred had said.

"Let's teach them a lesson," Fred suggested suddenly, standing up as he spoke.

"Yeah," Louie agreed with a smile as he realized what Fred had in mind. Ralph stood up as well and followed the boys even though he had no idea what they were doing.

"Heh-heh," Louie chuckled as he picked Daniel's pants and shirt off the ground. "This is going to be real funny."

"Look at this," Fred remarked, picking up Lynn's clothes and showing them to the others. "She even dresses like a boy."

"Maybe it's 'cuz they're twins," Ralph suggested.

"What does that got to do with anything?" Fred shot back.

"Uh, I don't know," Ralph mumbled, hanging his head in embarrassment.

"We'd better get out of here, Fred," Louie suggested.

"Yeah, let's go," Ralph agreed.

The boys took one last look at Lynn and Daniel who were still splashing each other in the water. They chuckled and ran off into the woods carrying Lynn and Daniel's clothes with them.

"What was that?" Daniel said suddenly. He abruptly stopped splashing and turned his head towards the woods.

"What?" Lynn threw in one last splash right in Daniel's face.

"I thought I saw somebody," Daniel replied, ignoring the water in his eyes. "Over there, by our clothes."

"Who?" Lynn asked nervously. She had stopped splashing and was looking around the woods intently, trying to see any movement in the trees.

"I don't know," Daniel answered. "But they ran away really fast."

"We'd better get out," Lynn suggested.

"Yeah," Daniel agreed.

The twins swam slowly back to the shore. Even though they were both nervous about someone being around, they did not want to make any noise and attract attention. Lynn tried swimming underwater as fast as she could, but when she came up for air she found that she was no farther ahead of Daniel. As they approached the shore, both of them realized that something was wrong.

"Our clothes!" Daniel shouted in panic, running around on the shore. His eyes desperately searched the grass, the trees, the bushes, and everywhere else. "Our clothes are gone!"

"What?" Lynn cried, turning her head and trying to see if maybe their clothes were lying somewhere else.

"I told you someone would see us!" Daniel cried angrily.

"But who would take our clothes?" Lynn wondered aloud. "Even if someone did see us, they wouldn't be mean enough to..." Her voice trailed off as she realized what must have happened.

"Fred!" they both shouted together. It had to be him. He had been mean to them ever since he came to town last year with his dad and mom. No matter what Lynn and Daniel did, whether it was trying to include him in a game of checkers or bringing fresh baked cookies over to his house, he always acted as if he hated them. He managed to steal their friends Louie and Ralph. The three of them became Lynn and Daniel's worst enemies. It was like some nightmare fairy tale about a wicked sorcerer coming to ruin their lives.

"Why does he always torment us?" Lynn cried in frustration. "We try so hard to be nice to him."

"I don't know," Daniel replied. "Maybe it's because of his parents. They never talk to us and the father gives me the coldest stares."

"I know what you mean," Lynn agreed. "One time when I was walking near their house, he stared at me the whole time and never once waved or smiled. He turned away and went into his house like he didn't want to even look at me."

"Hmmm," Daniel nodded as he turned his attention to the ground. He had been listening to his sister and looking around the area at the same time. "Look at this," he pointed to the ground, "I think they left a trail."

"Where?" Lynn cried as she rushed over to where Daniel was pointing. She was still dripping water all over and her body was covered with goose bumps from the cold air.

"Right there," Daniel pointed as he also began to shiver. "I think I see a footprint."

"Y-yeah," Lynn agreed, rubbing her bare arms to stay warm. "And look, it goes off this way."

"Let's follow it," Daniel suggested.

"O.K.," Lynn replied.

They entered the woods with their heads down and their hands crossed on their arms, trying to stay warm. The footprints were everywhere and Daniel found his sock stuck to a tree branch along the way.

"Shhhh," Daniel cried suddenly, lifting his finger to his lips and holding up his left hand to stop Lynn. "I think I hear something."

Lynn stood quietly next to her brother and listened to the birds and the wind and the crickets that were just now beginning to make their nighttime music in the fading daylight. She stopped rubbing her arms so that she could focus all of her attention on listening.

"You hear that?" Daniel whispered.

"I think so," Lynn replied, although she really wasn't sure she heard anything out of the ordinary.

"It sounds like laughter," Daniel suggested.

Lynn listened a little more.

"Yeah," she said after a moment's hesitation. "It does."

"It's coming from over there," Daniel pointed. "C'mon."

Daniel waved his sister on and the two of them crept slowly through the woods towards the sound of the laughter. It definitely sounded like boys, and the closer they got, the more sure they were that it was Fred, Louie, and Ralph.

"I wish we could have stayed to see the looks on their faces," Lynn heard Louie say. The twins had crept close enough to clearly hear everything. Daniel motioned with his hand and the two of them crouched behind a nearby bush. About ten feet away, Fred, Louie, and Ralph were sitting on a log laughing and talking. Lynn craned her head to the left and saw their clothes lying in a small pile in front of the boys. She tapped Daniel on the shoulder and pointed.

"Mmm," Daniel mumbled. He nodded his head to indicate that he saw the clothes as well.

"We had to leave," Fred responded to Louie's comment. He had no idea that he was being watched. "They might have seen us. And this way they'll have to walk all the way home in their underwear."

The boys all laughed heartily as they imagined Lynn and Daniel walking down the road half-naked.

"And then," Fred continued with a wicked smile, "someone might see them and tell the whole town about the twins who go swimming together in their underwear!"

The boys laughed again. Ralph's laugh was a little less hearty as if he was not sure why he was laughing.

"And then," Fred went on between laughs. He held his belly with his hands and had trouble talking, "and then, when the other neighbors find out, they'll make those twins feel so ashamed they'll have to move away."

Fred burst into laughter again. Louie laughed but he couldn't help staring at Fred in confusion. What was he talking about? This was all just a fun prank.

Lynn looked at Daniel in fear and he too was shocked. They never realized just how much Fred despised them. What kind of a monster was he?

"I don't want them to leave," Ralph interrupted.

Fred continued laughing. Louie sat back quietly and watched Fred.

"I like them," Ralph continued.

"Like them?" Fred repeated. He stopped laughing immediately and stared coldly at Ralph. "Like them? How can you like them?"

"They're nice," Ralph said simply.

"They're sick!" Fred shouted. "Look at what they were just doing! A brother and sister swimming in public in their underwear."

"I sometimes go swimming in my underwear," Ralph commented.

"Not with a girl," Fred attacked. "Especially a weird girl like her. You ever see how she acts so much like a boy? She and her brother play around and act like two brothers."

"That's for sure," Louie agreed. "I hardly ever see her wearing a dress. And I think Daniel does more cooking than she does."

"Ain't that 'cuz their daddy went off and joined the war?" Ralph asked innocently.

"Just how stupid are you?" Fred shouted. "Just 'cause the daddy's gone don't mean that Daniel's gotta act like the mommy."

"Don't call me stupid," Ralph warned.

"You are stupid," Fred shot back.

"I'm warning you," Ralph said.

"Stupid, stupid, stupid, stupid," Fred teased.

"Aaaah!" Ralph roared as he ran at Fred. Louie backed out of the way just in time as Ralph jumped on top of Fred and wrestled him to the ground.

"Now's our chance!" Daniel whispered, grabbing Lynn's arm and pulling her up. "Let's go!"

The twins jumped out of the bushes and ran to their clothes. Ralph and Fred were so busy wrestling on the ground that they did not even notice them. But Louie, who was standing to the side watching the fight, saw them immediately.

"Hey!" he shouted as Lynn reached down to grab her shirt. "It's them!"

Lynn stood up with all of her clothes in her arms and stared at the boys. Fred and Ralph stopped fighting and looked up from the ground to see what was going on.

"Get them!" Fred shouted.

Lynn and Daniel turned and ran. Louie leaped after them but stumbled over Fred who was trying to get out of Ralph's grip.

"Let go, let go," Fred shouted at Ralph. "They're getting away!"

Ralph rolled over slowly as Fred pushed him with all his strength. "C'mon!" he shouted in frustration.

Louie pulled Fred up and they took off after Daniel and Lynn. They never would have had a chance of catching the twins if it had been a normal race. Daniel was one of the fastest boys around and Lynn was even faster. Normally, the two skinny twins could have easily darted in and out of the trees and given their pursuers the slip. But this time, with their clothes bunched up in their arms, they couldn't run at top speed because their hands were not free to move the branches out of their way. They had to bend down and circle wide around any big tree or bush.

"Split up!" Daniel commanded when the boys were almost upon them.

Lynn ran off to the left and Daniel to the right. Fred and Louie paused for a minute, then turned and chased Daniel.

"Get him, get him, get him," Fred urged Louie, who was just a little ahead of him.

Daniel turned and hid behind a huge rock. Louie saw him turn and ran right towards him. Then, without warning, Daniel shot his leg out from behind the rock and Louie went flying forward, landing on the ground with a thud. Daniel looked down at him and smiled.

"Gotcha, you creep!" Fred cried from the other side of the rock as he grabbed Daniel's arm. "You thought you were so smart."

The clothes fell out of Daniel's hands and he struggled to pull his arm free.

"Let go!" he demanded.

"No way," Fred replied. "Not after that stunt you just pulled on Louie." Fred turned his head towards his friend. "You okay, Louie?"

"I guess so," Louie answered as he got up slowly and wiped the dust and dirt off his pants. "No thanks to you," he glared at Daniel.

"Hey, I'm sorry," Daniel began, "but you guys were chasing us. You stole our clothes and left us practically naked back there."

"So?" Fred responded. "It was just a prank. That don't give you the right to almost kill Louie."

"I didn't almost kill him!" Daniel argued.

"Sure you did," Louie growled as he approached Daniel. Fred was still holding Daniel's arm and trying to grab the other one as well. "I could have smashed my head against a tree or a rock."

"Serves you right," Daniel said. "What did you expect? That I'd just sit back and let you steal our clothes and then give them back to you when you chased us?"

"You jerk!" Louie cried as he punched Daniel in the stomach. All of the air was pushed out of Daniel's lungs and he fell to his knees trying to breathe. Fred kicked him in the face.

Daniel struggled to get up as Louie and Fred stood over him smiling. They knew they had him outnumbered.

"Hey!" a voice shouted from behind. Fred turned just in time to see Lynn's fist heading towards his face. It smashed him right in the nose and he fell to the ground with his hands covering his face.

"My nose!" Fred cried as the blood began to pour out.

"Lynn!" Daniel cried. He looked up to see his sister standing there angrily, her fists at the ready and her hair still dripping wet. She was actually a pretty scary sight, standing there in her underwear like some crazy woman ready to tear them apart.

"Leave him alone!" she shouted.

Louie looked nervously at Lynn, then over at Daniel, and finally at Fred who was still lying on the ground wiping the blood from his nose. He stood there, fidgeting, unsure of what to do next. The odds were even now.

Fred stood up and joined him. Blood was still flowing out of his nose and he kept sniffling, trying to stop it. Lynn cautiously made her way over to her brother.

"Are you alright?" she asked him.

"Yeah, fine," Daniel answered, standing up next to his sister. "These guys just caught me by surprise is all."

"Well?" Lynn said, turning towards Fred and Ralph with her fists still at the ready. "Are we going to continue this or are you just going to let us go?"

"I ain't going to fight no girl," Fred said bitterly. "You may have caught me by surprise but I ain't going to hit you back. At least I know how a girl is supposed to act."

Lynn glared at him. She really wanted to fight. It was the first time in a long time that she felt good about herself. She was free. The air was blowing over her wet skin, making her goose bumps stand out. Her blood was pumping. Her body was tingling with anticipation and excitement. It felt great to be alive.

"C'mon, Louie," Fred commanded, turning away from the twins, "let's leave these two freaks in the woods."

Chapter 2
Decisions

"You really went crazy back there," Daniel commented to Lynn once they had gotten dressed and begun to walk home. The sun was on its way down and they had to hustle along the dirt road if they were going to make it home before dark. "I actually thought you were going to fight them."

"So?" Lynn shot back. "We could have taken them."

"That's not what I mean," Daniel replied. "You shouldn't have tried to fight them in the first place."

"Why?" Lynn snapped. She couldn't believe her own brother was just like all the other boys. "Because I'm a girl?"

"Yeah," Daniel answered. He could tell by the anger in Lynn's voice that she was ready to explode and he regretted having started the conversation.

"I can't believe you're saying this!" Lynn shouted. She stopped walking and turned towards her brother. "I can't believe you think like all the other boys."

"I don't think like all the other boys," Daniel defended himself. "I just think that..."

"You think that girls shouldn't fight," she finished for him. "You think that they belong in the house and in the shadows, better seen and not heard."

"No, I don't," Daniel argued. He hated when she finished his sentences and put words into his mouth. "You know I think that girls are just as smart as boys. I'd be crazy not to. Heck, you're just as smart as I am."

"And as fast," Lynn added.

"Yeah," Daniel agreed.

"And as tough," she added again.

"That's for sure," Daniel chuckled a little.

"Then what's the problem?" Lynn wondered.

"You just can't go out there acting like a boy," Daniel answered.

Lynn hung her head. She knew what Daniel was about to say. They had had this conversation many times in the past. Lynn would complain, Daniel would remind her what the rest of the world thought of girls. Lynn would argue a little, complain and moan, but eventually she would agree that Daniel was right. Women were treated differently from men and there wasn't anything she could do about it.

"Look, Lynn, I'm sorry," Daniel said slowly, lifting up her chin with his finger so that she was looking at him. "I know how much you want to be yourself and show the rest of the world what you can do. But you just can't."

Tears were beginning to form in Lynn's eyes.

"I hate it too," Daniel continued, trying to make her understand just how much pain he felt when he saw his sister cry. He really did think it was unfair. Lynn was just as smart as he was. He knew she could do whatever she wanted to if it weren't for all these stupid rules you had to live by. "But think about what the neighbors are going to say now."

Lynn looked up at him nervously.

"Fred will surely go tell everyone what happened," Daniel continued, "and then they will know that you punched him and wanted to fight."

Lynn's eyes opened wide and her jaw lowered. "What do you think they will do?" she asked.

"I don't know," Daniel replied. "Maybe nothing. But they sure as heck will give us lots of grief every time we see them."

"Oh God," Lynn moaned as she thought about all the teasing and name calling she would have to endure.

"Yeah," Daniel agreed. "It isn't going to be pretty."

"I'm sorry, Daniel," Lynn said sincerely.

"Awww, don't worry about it," Daniel replied as he began to walk again. It was almost dark now. "After all, you did save my skin."

Lynn smiled and began walking as well. He really was a great brother.

As they approached the house they could sense that something was wrong. There was a strange silence in the air, as if the birds and crickets had all left the area. The wind was still and the full moon overhead gave off just enough light to bathe the house in an eerie white glow.

"Why aren't there any lights on?" Daniel wondered aloud.

"I don't know," Lynn replied. "I'm sure Grandmother's home. She was napping when we left."

"Maybe she's still asleep," Daniel suggested.

"Maybe," Lynn agreed.

The twins walked into the yard and towards the front porch. It was a relatively large house for the three of them that seemed even larger since their father had gone off to fight in the war. He had left only a couple of months ago when the call went out from Augusta that the 3rd Maine Regiment was forming. Lynn and Daniel had protested, saying that he couldn't leave them all alone. He had argued that he would only be gone a few months and that their grandmother would be more than capable of handling everything.

She was a sharp old woman with a fiery personality and a sense of humor that would often leave the whole family rolling on the floor laughing hysterically. Lynn couldn't believe how quick her grandmother's mind was for someone who was over sixty. She remembered every detail and fact that she was exposed to. This made her great at arguments, especially ones that concerned politics. She could have been a lawyer or a senator if only she had been fortunate enough to have been born a man.

"Hey," Daniel whispered as his eyes strained to see ahead of him, "is that Grandmother sitting on the porch?"

Lynn squinted as well. "I think it is," she replied.

"What's she doing sitting there in the dark?"

The twins slowed their pace a little and walked towards the porch. They weren't sure if their grandmother was asleep or not. They hoped she was since it would be better if she didn't know how late they got back. Daniel picked up the lantern that they kept at the porch step and lit it.

"Grandmother?" Lynn whispered softly as the dim yellow light illuminated the porch. The old woman's eyes were definitely open but she was staring blankly into the darkness. Lynn felt a sudden panic. Was she dead?

"Grandmother?" Daniel tried again. She still did not respond. He looked on the floor near her chair and saw a newspaper lying in a heap. He bent down to pick it up.

"He's gone," their grandmother mumbled before Daniel could look at the paper. The sudden sound split the stillness in the air and surprised the twins. They jumped back and stared at their grandmother.

Lynn took a deep breath and covered her mouth with her hands. Her eyes began to well up with tears as she realized immediately that their grandmother was referring to their father.

"What?" Daniel cried. He began to shuffle through the paper, looking for what she had seen.

"They called it Bull Run," Grandmother continued. Her voice showed no emotion and her body was stiff and unmoving. It was like all the life had been drained from her.

"It was supposed to be a great victory," she said. "Our glorious army was supposed to march into the South and show them the error of their ways."

Daniel found the page listing the local men killed in the battle and scanned its contents. His eyes darted back and forth nervously.

"But it wasn't glorious," Grandmother continued. "It was a disaster. Our men ran like a stampede of cattle, trampling each other as they went. The rebels just had to stand there and fire."

"Oh no," Daniel whispered as his eyes stopped scanning. He handed the paper to Lynn. "There he is: Leonard Rhodes, 3rd Maine Regiment."

Lynn looked down in horror as she
father's name in black letters halfway down
She began to sob.

Daniel reached out and pulled Lynn towards
The newspaper fell to the ground.

"Oh Daniel," Lynn cried between sobs. Her chest
was heaving and her breath came in spurts. "What are
we going to do now?"

Daniel continued to hold Lynn tight as he rubbed
her back with his hands. He looked up into the dark
sky and thought about their father. They had been like
buddies. Ever since their mother died, Lynn and Daniel
found their father to be open and caring and kind to
them. He had played with them, talked with them, and
spent every spare moment he had with them. Daniel
was even looking forward to the day when they would
be old enough to all go out to a local tavern together
and chat like old friends.

That won't ever happen now, Daniel thought bitterly. Tears began to flow down his face.

The two of them stood on the porch quietly for
several minutes. Lynn had stopped sobbing and was
now crying quietly in Daniel's arms. He was still holding her tight and letting himself cry. It felt good to let
all of his anger, sadness, and bitterness out. It was funny
in a way, really. Lynn had always felt comfortable being herself and acting like a boy around Daniel for as
long as he could remember. Now he realized that he
too could be himself and let his feelings out around
her just as easily. He felt no shame at crying and in
fact, he even felt good.

The tears finally stopped and they stood holding
each other quietly. Daniel looked back up into the sky,
thought for a moment, then looked back down.

"I've got to go, Lynn," he said.

"What?" Lynn cried, pushing away from him and staring into his face. "Go where?"

"To the war," Daniel replied. "I've got to join up and help."

"Huh? B-but why?" Lynn stuttered nervously.

"I've just got to," Daniel said simply. "Dad would have wanted me to."

"But what about me?" Lynn wondered aloud. She was beginning to panic as she realized that not only would she be alone, but that she might also lose her brother to the war as well.

"You'll be fine here with Grandmother," Daniel said, looking down at their grandmother who was still sitting in the chair. She had finally shown interest in what the twins were saying and had begun to stand up.

"But I don't want to stay with Grandmother," Lynn protested. "I want to be with you!"

"Lynn, please," Daniel begged. "Don't make this any harder than it is. I don't want to leave you either."

"Then don't!" Lynn shouted. She had begun to cry again and was getting angry as well. "Why do you have to run off and fight? What makes this so important that you have to leave us?"

"C'mon, Lynn," Daniel said impatiently. "You know how important this war is. It could mean the end of the country forever."

"So?" she shouted back. "It's just a stupid country. It's not alive. I'm your twin—your last family member. If you leave me, then you leave the family. You destroy everything!"

"Stop this, Lynn!" Grandmother interrupted in a firm voice. It was a voice the twins had never heard her use before. She had always seemed meek and kind, never wanting to interfere with their father and how he raised the children. Now, all of sudden, she was a strong, dominating woman who seemed angry enough to eat rocks.

"You're acting like a child!" Grandmother scolded. "Crying and screaming and worrying about yourself and how you'll feel. Daniel here is about to do a brave thing, a thing your father would be proud of. He's honoring your father's terrible sacrifice while you are only thinking about yourself!"

Lynn hung her head and stared at her feet. "I'm sorry, Grandmother," she said softly. "I just don't wanna lose my brother too."

"We all lose someone," Grandmother replied a little softer this time. She placed her hand on Lynn's shoulder. "But it is how we deal with that loss that matters. Now, you can cry and weep and fuss about your loss or you can be like your brother here and do something positive to honor your father."

"L-like what?" Lynn asked softly. She had no idea what Grandmother was getting at. She was only sixteen, just a girl. What could she do?

"Well," Grandmother said slowly. She sat back down in her chair and put her hand on her chin as if she were thinking. Lynn waited anxiously for her to continue, wondering what this wonderful old lady had in mind.

"I've heard that many women are starting up soldier's aid societies," she began. "They are raising money for the soldiers, recruiting men, and even sewing and baking for them."

Lynn lowered her head. Grandmother didn't seem to be as creative as Lynn thought.

"But somehow I don't think that would suit you," Grandmother continued. Lynn's hopes shot up again. "You're too rough and bullish to work well with other girls. You'd probably be in a fight before the first day."

Lynn and Daniel smiled.

"Soooo," Grandmother dragged the word out, trying to be as dramatic as possible. "Why don't you go ahead and join up with your brother?"

"Join up?" both Daniel and Lynn repeated together in a shout.

"Why not?" Grandmother asked innocently. "Lynn fights as good as any boy I've ever seen."

"But she's a girl!" Daniel protested. "Girls can't join the army."

"Of course they can't," Grandmother said impatiently. "But who needs to know she's a girl?"

"You mean disguise myself?" Lynn said softly. The idea started to sound interesting.

"Of course," Grandmother answered simply. Her voice made it sound as if it was the most obvious thing in the world. "It wouldn't be the first time that a woman has had to pretend that she was a man to get something."

"But that's dishonest," Daniel protested. He wasn't sure how to react. This was the craziest idea he had ever heard. Sure, Lynn could pass as a boy if she cut her hair and wrapped up her chest, but how long could she do that?

"And with Daniel as your twin," Grandmother continued, ignoring Daniel's comment, "he could help you at times when things got awkward."

"Like if I need to bathe?" Lynn suggested.

"Sure," Grandmother smiled. "You're sure to be put in the same company. And when you join up you'll just say your name is Larry instead of Lynn and that you and Daniel are twins."

"Hold it, hold it, hold it," Daniel interrupted, raising his hands in an effort to stop the conversation. "Why are you acting so crazy, Grandmother? You can't actually believe that we would do something like this!"

"Crazy?" Grandmother raised her voice. "Crazy? Don't ever call me crazy, young man!"

Daniel took a step back. He had never seen their grandmother like this. Ever since they had known her, she had been a quiet, caring old lady. Once in a while he had seen her angry, especially that time that Lynn and he had dipped all her underwear in the ink wells. But that was different than this. She was acting possessed, as if something in her past was coming back to haunt her.

"What's crazy, young man, is the way I've been treated since I was a little girl," Grandmother shouted. Her hands flew in the air and her face burned with emotion. Daniel could almost swear he saw tears forming in her eyes. "I was smarter and quicker than anyone in my family or town, but because I was a girl, no one would give me a chance. I spent my whole life seeing stupid men who couldn't debate themselves out of a paper bag passing me by and running my life. What's crazy is this whole stupid society you men have set up and now that Lynn has a chance to contribute to a war that men have started, you tell me that I'm crazy?!"

"I...I didn't mean—," Daniel tried to say.

"You never mean to," Grandmother snapped, as if she had heard that before. She seemed so enraged, yet her anger was not directed at Daniel but at the world. She wasn't even looking at him. "You men just continue doing what you're doing, never even noticing how you hurt us. It's as if we don't exist, or worse that we exist only for your enjoyment."

Neither Daniel nor Lynn responded. They were afraid to. They stood silently, waiting for Grandmother to continue.

"All my life...," she said slowly. Her voice was sad now and she spoke much softer. Her eyes were staring straight ahead, as if she were reliving events in her head. "All my life I have wanted to do more. But they never would let me—my father, my mother, the teachers, the neighbors, even my sisters. They all told me that girls didn't do that. That the world did not work that way. They never let me do anything."

She took several deep breaths. She looked around. She looked down at the newspaper again and her face seemed to change. The energy left her and she looked sad again.

"I'm sorry, Daniel," Grandmother finally said softly. "You didn't mean to insult me. That's just the way it is. I know it's not your fault, Grandson."

Lynn had never seen her grandmother like this before. What fire, what energy and drive she had. It truly was a crime that she was never allowed to do anything besides be a housewife.

"I'm going to do it, Grandmother!" Lynn shouted excitedly. "I'm not going to let my life be forever ruled by men. I'm going to go fight for what I believe in—and let them just try and stop me."

She looked over at Daniel to see his reaction. He rolled his eyes and looked away. What could he do?

Chapter 3

The Ladies Aid Society

Mary closed another package and looked around the room. Boxes were everywhere—in piles on the floor, stacked up neatly against a wall, or even lying in the hallway. Some were half-opened, waiting to be packed for the soldiers at the front. Other boxes were already closed and being labeled by Mrs. Anderson or Mrs. Black, the lady who owned the house. Next to Mary was her little sister Helen, still working on packing up the jellies Mary had given her over a half-hour ago. She seemed to not care how fast she worked and would often stare at the ceiling, looking for some unknown pattern. Mary wondered if it was a mistake bringing Helen. After all, she was only nine years old and didn't really understand what it was they were doing.

The girls had started coming to Mrs. Black's house over a year ago. When the war began, Mary had wanted to help in some way. She had always been interested in what was going on around the country. When she was in school she would spend extra time reading about history, especially anything dealing with slavery. As a young girl, she remembered her parents attending anti-slavery meetings and even helping fugitive slaves. Then, when the South fired on Fort Sumter and started the war, she couldn't wait to get involved.

But when everyone started signing up and organizing committees to help, they all forgot about her. She was just a teenage girl, they said. What could she do to help?

Within a few weeks, her uncle and cousins all went off to fight, leaving her alone with her mean aunt and even meaner girl cousins. She hated spending time with them. As soon as she finished her chores, she would run to join Mrs. Black and the other volunteers in the neighborhood. She heard about the work one day while eavesdropping on someone's conversation in church. They were discussing how much the government needed supplies and what was being done about it. Mary quickly jumped at the chance to get involved and by the end of the month she was a welcome member of Mrs. Black's staff.

It was actually a common thing for the women in Frankford, Pennsylvania, and nearby Philadelphia to organize soldier's aid societies. After all, war was only partly fought by the soldiers on the front. They couldn't fight without the food, clothing, and supplies from back home. Women throughout the country had realized this and formed groups to organize and distribute supplies to the hundreds of thousands of soldiers in the armies. Several major groups in Philadelphia had already begun sending things to the front. Women from all around the city donated their time and energy to collecting and producing materials for the soldiers to use. Mary sewed socks, shirts, pads, and cushions for the soldiers to lie on. She baked cookies and packed boxes of eggs, crackers, green tea, pickles, and even port wine to send to the soldiers. Although it wasn't the same as fighting, she knew the things they sent to the soldiers reminded the men of how much they were cared for and made their job a little easier. Besides, working in the house with other women kept Mary from thinking about how lonely she was.

"How is it going, Mary?" Mrs. Black asked as she approached the younger girl. Even though Mary was only fourteen, she looked much older than many of the other girls in town. That was probably why Mrs. Black had agreed so quickly to let Mary help. Of course by now, with the war going so badly, just about any girl who wanted to help was allowed to. Mary even brought her little sister Helen once in a while.

"Pretty well," Mary answered. "I've finished the pickles and I was about to help Helen with the last of the jellies."

"Wonderful," Mrs. Black replied. She let out a sigh, sat down in a chair near Mary, and placed her hands in her lap. She was a large woman with broad shoulders and long dark hair that flowed down her back. Her hands were ragged and cut from all of the packing and her voice was deep and raspy from all the recruiting of favors she did around town. "That makes over twenty boxes stuffed today. With the ten we did yesterday that should be more than enough to satisfy Mrs. Jones."

"Did she ask for more again today?" Mary wondered. She had never met Mrs. Jones or the other leading women in the Philadelphia Aid Society but she had always wanted to. They were such a small group of women, yet they managed to organize so much.

"No," Mrs. Black answered. "She's too busy. But she sent us a copy of one of Mrs. Harris' letters describing the front."

"She did?" Mrs. Anderson interrupted from across the room. She was the opposite of Mrs. Black, small and petite with a high-pitched voice that quickly got annoying. She stopped sewing the socks she was working on and joined Mary and Mrs. Black. "I never read it. What did it say?"

"She discussed the horrible conditions of the hospitals," Mrs. Black replied with a shudder, "if you can call them that. I still can't believe that our government is doing so little to clean them up."

"It's a good thing we're here," Mary added with a smile. She took any chance she could get to remind herself of the importance of what she was doing. "Without us, who knows how many more men would be dying."

"That's for sure," agreed Mrs. Anderson. "It's bad enough that thousands of men are being killed in battles, but to lose even more to starvation and disease is almost a crime."

"I'm finished, Mary," Helen interrupted. Everyone turned to see Helen standing next to another box of jellies and smiling broadly.

"Good job, Helen," Mrs. Black cried enthusiastically, clapping her hands. "You certainly have been a big help today."

"I'm glad Mary brought you," added Mrs. Anderson. Helen smiled. Her cheeks turned almost as red as her long auburn hair and she turned away.

"Thank you," she said bashfully.

Knock-knock-knock! A hand tapped lightly on the door outside.

"Mary, would you get that please?" Mrs. Black asked politely.

"Certainly," Mary answered as she headed towards the door.

"Hi, Mrs. Garasic," Mary said to the figure in the doorway. "What took you so long? We were expecting you over an hour ago."

"I found some disturbing news," Mrs. Garasic replied somberly as she walked into the room and sat next to Mrs. Black. Her curly black hair was messy and her eyes were red as if she had been crying. In her hand, she held a letter, and when she looked into Mrs. Black's eyes it was with a strong feeling of sadness and pain. It frightened everyone.

"What is it?" Mrs. Black asked nervously. She was afraid to listen but knew she had to. Her husband and Mrs. Garasic's were in the same company in the Army of the Potomac and they always shared each other's letters. All the women would listen intently to the words from the front whether they were battle descriptions or everyday accounts of what the soldiers had done that day. Lately, Mr. Black had neglected to write his wife and she found that she had to get all of her news from Mrs. Garasic.

"I don't know how to begin," Mrs. Garasic answered. Her voice was shaky and her hands trembled uncontrollably.

"Carol," Mrs. Black said softly as she took the other woman's hand in her own. "Take your time. It's O.K. We're all friends here. There's no reason to hide your feelings."

Mrs. Garasic looked up. Her body shuddered once and her face twitched. She still was unsure how to begin.

"Just read the letter, Carol," Mrs. Black urged.

"Oh, O.K.," Mrs. Garasic said softly. She opened the letter and began reading. Mary reached for Helen's soft little hand and held it tight.

"Dear Carol," Mrs. Garasic began.

"I don't know how to tell you this. I don't even know how to explain it. I can't explain it to myself. It's all so crazy, so utterly crazy. Every day, I wake up and try to ready myself for the coming battle only to find that yet another comrade has succumbed to some mysterious disease or sickness. How, dear Lord, can we fight the rebels when we spend so much time just fighting to stay alive?"

"It's even worse than Mrs. Harris described it," Mrs. Anderson interrupted.

"Remember how I told you," Mrs. Garasic continued after a moment's hesitation, *"last month that diarrhea and dysentery had swept through the regiment? Well, even before that was over, typhoid began spreading through the army like a fire in a dry forest. No one seemed to be immune. It struck the officers, the regulars like me, the cooks, the medical staff and even the supply people. Whole regiments have been quarantined and prevented from doing anything."*

"What's typhoid?" Helen interrupted.

"It's a terrible disease that kills lots of people," Mary whispered. "Now be quiet. I'll tell you more later."

"It has been awful," Mrs. Garasic was still reading. *"Men I once looked upon as being strong, hardy individuals are reduced to screaming, groaning, and crying out in pain. They run high fevers, sweat, scream of stomach pains, and bleed in places I don't care to describe.*

"Fortunately, the terrible sickness has passed me over, but not all of our friends have been so lucky. You

probably have noticed that John [Mrs. Black's husband], has not written Nancy [Mrs. Black] lately. It's not because he has gotten lazy or does not care for her anymore. Lord knows his devotion to her is sometimes beyond understanding. But even his love and dedication could not overpower this terrible disease."

Mrs. Black gasped and fell backwards into her chair. Her eyes began to swell with tears. "No," she whispered.

"I've watched as he has struggled to stay awake." Mrs. Garasic's voice cracked as she continued reading. Her heart felt sick and she wanted to run and hide. She hated being the one to have to break the news but she had no choice. *"He has tried so hard to not give in to the pain and weakness. The doctors even gave him turpentine and quinine, but nothing seemed to help. Only the whiskey provided some relief to him, but of course that prevented him from writing or doing anything else.*

"Carol, I am not sure what to tell you or how to advise you. There is nothing else we can do. But Nancy needs to know. She needs to hear how much her husband has been calling for her, how much he has cried out his love for her."

Mrs. Garasic took a deep breath and rushed on. Mrs. Black was still shaking her head back and forth, muttering "No, no."

"I don't want Nancy to find out about this in the newspaper. I want her to know that her husband died with her name on his lips. Tell her what I've said. Tell her how much he meant to us and how much she meant to him. I know it will pain you to do this but you must.

Take care, my love. I will write you again soon.

All my love,

Anthony."

"Nooo!" Mrs. Black cried as Mrs. Garasic lowered the letter and looked across at her.

"No! No! No! No!" she screamed, standing up and throwing the chair backwards in anger and grief. "It can't be! Not like this, not now!"

Mrs. Garasic, Mrs. Anderson, Mary, and Helen all stood quietly and watched.

"How?" she cried. "How could the Lord do this to me? Does he think it's funny? Does he have some strange sense of humor? Does he think that killing my husband with disease is a good way to punish me when I have spent so much time and energy trying to help keep the soldiers clean and happy?"

She looked around the room at the many boxes packed up and sealed for the trip to the front.

"Look at this!" she shouted, with a wave of her hand. "Look at all this! Shirts to keep them dry, socks to keep them warm, cushions for their heads, jellies for their pleasure, tea for their health, and eggs for their strength. It's all worthless!" she cried angrily. She ran to the nearest box and knocked it to the floor. "Worthless!" she repeated.

"Nancy, no!" Mrs. Anderson cried.

"Worthless!" Mrs. Black shouted again, tipping over another box. The socks rolled out onto the floor. Mrs. Black grabbed one of the balled up socks. "Socks!" She shouted as she threw it across the room. "Socks! What good are they? Will they stop the fighting?"

"And tea?" she cried, picking up several bags of tea and showing them to the ladies. "How will this stop the war? Will it stop a rebel march?" she yelled angrily as she took one of the bags and threw it against the wall. It smashed flat at the impact and sent tea shooting everywhere. "Will it make the secessionists run in fear?" She threw another bag against the wall. "Will it cure diarrhea?" She threw another bag. "Will it cure typhoid?" She threw another and another.

"Nancy, stop!" Mrs. Garasic commanded, grabbing Mrs. Black by the shoulders and spinning her around. "You're ruining everything!"

Mrs. Black turned around angrily, still holding bags of tea in her hand. She paused for a moment.

"This won't bring back John," Mrs. Garasic reminded her.

Pain washed over Mrs. Black's face. Instantly, her anger changed to terrible grief. Tears burst from her eyes and she fell into Mrs. Garasic's arms.

"Oh Carol!" she sobbed.

Mrs. Garasic held Mrs. Black tight and patted her back. "It's O.K.," she consoled her through her own tears. "We understand."

Mary and Helen stood by awkwardly and listened to Mrs. Black sob. It felt strange standing by themselves and watching the older women deal with their grief. Even though these nice ladies had treated Mary like one of them, she still was only a girl and they tended to ignore her at times like this. It made Mary realize that no matter how hard she tried, she would never belong with them. She wanted to reach out and hug Mrs. Black. She wanted to tell her that she knew how it felt to lose someone you love. She wanted to remind her how important their work was. But she couldn't. She didn't belong. She was just a girl and they wouldn't listen to her.

"C'mon, Helen," Mary said quietly. She grabbed Helen's hand again and headed towards the door. Mrs. Black was still sobbing in Mrs. Garasic's arms while Mrs. Anderson patted her back. "Let's leave them alone."

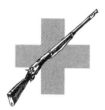

Chapter 4
Something Better

Several days passed but Mary still could not shake the feelings of loneliness and uselessness. She didn't understand why everyone she cared about had left her alone. First her mother and father had died while on a trip to Kansas. Then, after the war began, her uncle and cousins had gone off to fight. And now, when she finally felt that she was doing something important and making some friends, this had to happen.

Mrs. Black didn't come looking for her, and Mary made no attempt to go see her. The work in the aid society might continue but it would never be as energetic and positive now that the shadow of death hung directly over Mrs. Black's house. When Helen asked what was going on, Mary told her that it wasn't any of her concern and to forget it. Mary needed to think. She needed to figure out what to do with her life. She wanted to do something important and make a difference. Maybe it was too late to help the slaves as her parents had done, but she could still do something to help the North win the war. And perhaps even more, she wanted to get out of the house. She hated living with her cousins. They treated her like an unwanted dog who was only there to perform chores.

She walked out of the house to see her younger brother Thomas. He had returned from the army and was having a terrible time readjusting to life at home. As a young volunteer he had been totally unprepared for war and ran away from his regiment at the battle at Balls Bluff.[1] Everyone in the town, except Mary, had made fun of him and treated him like a terrible coward. While jealous of him for getting to leave home, Mary was not about to push away the only person in the family who still treated her with respect and love.

As she walked towards Thomas standing there in his beautiful blue soldier's uniform, Mary realized that she finally had a way out. Thomas could not stay home forever. He would have to return to the army. The townspeople were making his life miserable and teasing him for being a coward. Yesterday, the local bully's big dog, Taylor, had jumped on Thomas' little dog, Alfie, and started a fierce, brutal fight which ended in disaster. Now, after Thomas had buried his pet, he was going through more pain than Mary had ever seen. She knew that he would eventually have to face his fears and return to the army or else he would never be able to live with himself.

And when he does return, Mary thought to herself, *I can go with him!* She already knew of other women like Mrs. Harris from the Philadelphia Aid Society who went to the front to help. They distributed supplies, comforted the wounded, wrote letters for them, and did anything that was needed to make the men a little more comfortable. Of course Mary couldn't be a nurse. But she knew that if she showed up at a battlefield,

---

1. To find out more about why Thomas ran away and how he dealt with being branded a coward, read book four in the Young Heroes of History Series: *Nowhere to Turn.*

people would be so busy trying to take care of all the wounded and dead that no one would turn her away. It was a great idea, she realized. The thought made her happy again, happier than she had been for a long time. Finally, she would get to do something important. She skipped along the grass, but then quickly slowed down when she got close to her brother.

He stood quietly over the grave of his dog. It had been a vicious fight and Mary had done all she could to save Alfie's life. He had lost too much blood though and within a few hours of the fight he was dead.

"I'm sorry, Thomas," Mary said gently to him as she put her hand on his shoulder. She changed her mood completely to give Thomas as much sympathy as possible. "I know how much you loved him."

"Thanks," Thomas replied softly. He didn't feel like talking.

"I noticed you packed up your haversack," Mary added after an awkward silence. It was clear to her that Thomas did not want to talk about Alfie.

"Yeah," Thomas replied slowly. "I'm going back."

"To the regiment?" Mary wondered. *That was quicker than I expected,* she thought to herself.

"Yeah," Thomas said simply. "I got nothing left to stay for here. I might as well go."

"You're not going just because Alfie's dead, are you?" Mary asked. She was thrilled that Thomas had finally made a decision but she was concerned that he was running away from his troubles again.

"No," Thomas explained. "Not really. I've been thinking about what David said.[2] I've been thinking

---

2. David is his older brother who wrote him a letter from Georgia. For more information, consult book four, *Nowhere to Turn.*

about what you said. I've even been thinking about what the neighbors said."

Mary looked at him in surprise.

"I have been running," Thomas admitted. "I've been running from being picked on, running from my family, running from the farm, and running from the war. But I'm tired of running. I'm tired of feeling like a coward."

"You are not a coward," Mary said firmly.

"I know," Thomas agreed. His certainty surprised Mary. "I proved that to myself during the fight with Taylor [the bully's dog]. When something is really important to me, I don't run. I am as brave as anyone."

"I know," Mary said, smiling. "I've always known that. And I'm glad you know that too."

"I just wish Alfie didn't have to die for me to learn this," Thomas said sadly, staring down at the grave again.

"Me too," Mary said.

Thomas turned away from the grave and looked at Mary.

"Well, I guess this is goodbye," he said sadly.

"No, it's not," Mary argued. She tried really hard not to show her excitement. Thomas looked at her in confusion. There was a strange silence as Mary's mouth began to show a smirk.

"I'm going with you!" she explained.

"What?" Thomas exclaimed. "You can't go with me! I'm going off to fight!"

"I know that," Mary cried impatiently. "I'm not going to be a soldier, dummy. What did you think, that I would disguise myself as a man just to fight?"

"Well...I...uh," Thomas mumbled.

"Women don't have to dress up as men to help out in this war, you know," Mary began. She had heard the women in the aid society discuss this many times. It truly bothered them that some women felt that the only way to help was to pretend to not be a woman. It was a sore subject for Mary and she spoke as if she had said this many times in the past. There was an anger and bitterness in her voice that wasn't so much directed at Thomas as it was directed at the war in general. "Everyone seems to think that if you are not a soldier then you are not doing anything. They think only the fighting is what matters."

Thomas stood and listened. He knew better than to interrupt Mary when she was giving one of her speeches.

"Well, you boys couldn't fight without us," Mary continued after a short pause. "We make your clothes, organize your recruitment, clean your camps, and tend to the wounded."

"I know that, Mary," Thomas finally said. "Why are you telling me this now?"

"Because I'm tired of being here in Frankford," Mary whined. "We may be getting some things done but I want to do more."

"Like what?"

"I don't know," Mary responded. "Work for the Sanitary Commission, inspect the camps, help with the wounded. I don't know, just something more."

"You're not old enough to be a nurse."

"I know that," Mary replied. "But I'm old enough to help out. After all, if you can do it, why can't I?"

Thomas looked back at Mary. He didn't have any argument there. If he was in the army, why couldn't she help out too? She was older than he was and even if she was a girl, he had already seen and heard about women in the camps. They took care of the wounded and made sure that the camp was healthy. The way Mary always took care of his cuts and bruises, she'd be a natural.

"But what about Aunt Patricia?" Thomas suddenly realized. "What will she say?"

"What can she say?" Mary said smartly. "I'm not her daughter and she certainly doesn't treat me like she wants me around. She'll be glad to see me go."

She is probably right about that too, Thomas thought to himself. Aunt Patricia seemed to dislike Mary even more than Thomas. She always played favorites with her real daughters, Rachel and Jamie.

"Well, O.K.," Thomas said after a few more seconds of thinking. "I don't see any reason why you can't go. I probably couldn't stop you anyway and I could use some company."

"Hooray," Mary cheered as she jumped into Thomas' arms and hugged him. "Thank you, Thomas, thank you."

"You just gotta get lost when we get near my regiment," Thomas warned. He pushed Mary back and stared at her to show how serious he was.

"Don't worry," Mary said quickly. "As soon as we get near the troops, I'll go find the Sanitary Commission or hospital tent. No one will ever know your sister came with you."

Mary's home near Philadelphia and the location of the Battle of Antietam

Chapter 5

To the Front

The next day, Mary and Thomas set out to find Thomas' regiment. They knew that it would be difficult to locate since Thomas had been gone so long, but they were determined to get to the front as soon as possible. Neither of them could take another minute in their aunt's house. She grew meaner with each passing day and if they didn't get out soon, Mary was afraid she would explode.

Mary stuffed her toothbrush into her bag. It was already overpacked with bandages and other medical supplies she expected to need on her trip. She knew that there certainly wouldn't be any extra supplies available to her, and if she wanted to impress anyone she needed to be prepared.

"Whatcha doing?" Helen asked softly, approaching the table where Mary was working.

"Nothing," Mary lied. She still had not told Helen what was going on. She was afraid that she would cry and scream and make a scene when she found out that her older brother and sister were leaving her all alone.

"What's that bag for?" Helen asked innocently.

"Ummm," Mary mumbled.

"Are you going away?" Helen offered.

"Yes," Mary said softly. She couldn't lie to Helen. She loved her too much for that.

"Why?" Helen said simply. She still didn't seem that upset. Maybe she didn't understand what Mary was really doing.

"I'm going to help Thomas get back to his regiment," Mary decided to tell Helen. It was easier than the truth and it wasn't totally wrong. "He could use some help finding it and I want to make sure he gets there safely."

"How long will you be gone?" Helen wondered as her face began to show signs of worry.

"Oh, not that long," Mary answered. It would be easier for Helen if she thought Mary would be back soon. Once Mary arrived at the front, she could write Helen a letter and come back and visit on occasion.

"What about Mrs. Black?" Helen asked. "Won't she be upset?"

"Uh no," Mary replied. She was surprised that Helen had thought of Mrs. Black. Maybe she wasn't as unaware as Mary thought. "Mrs. Black knows that I am going and she even asked me to come back and tell her about what the army needs," Mary told Helen.

"Mary," Thomas interrupted as he walked into the room, "we really need to get going."

"I know, I know," Mary answered, closing up her bag and swinging it over her shoulder. "I was just saying goodbye to Helen."

Thomas looked down at his baby sister. She was the only one left in the family who had not been hurt by this terrible war. Her bright green eyes were sparkling and wide with curiosity and her laugh was still playful and filled with glee.

"Bye, Helen," Thomas said gently as he bent down to kiss her. "I'll miss you."

"I'll miss you too," Helen replied sadly. She reached out to hug her brother. She still only came up to his chest and he had to bend over to hug her. "Please come back soon," she said softly.

"I will, I will," Thomas replied firmly as he hugged her tight.

Mary watched her younger brother and sister holding each other tenderly and for the first time she began to wonder if they were doing the right thing. Thomas and Helen were the only ones she had left and they meant everything to her. The thought of something happening to Thomas was such a strong, terrible thought that she almost began to cry. It would be even worse for Helen. She would be devastated if anything happened to Thomas or her.

"Bye, Helen," Mary managed to say after she took a deep breath. She didn't want to think about these things. She wanted to say goodbye and get it over with. "I'll be back soon."

Helen and Mary hugged tight. Thomas stood by patiently. *One more minute won't matter,* he thought to himself.

They decided to take a train to Washington, D.C. Mary felt that the capital was the best place to start looking. Thomas' regiment was being reorganized along with the rest of the Army of the Potomac after the terrible disaster at the Battle of Second Bull Run. It seemed that whenever the Union generals led their men into battle they would always be outwitted by the cunning Southern generals who somehow managed to defeat the larger Union force. This time the defeat was large

The U.S. Capitol Building during the Civil War

National Archives

enough that wounded and dying soldiers lay in buildings all around the capital and the leaders of the army were being questioned and reassigned. Discouraged and enraged, President Lincoln decided to bring back General McClellan to lead the army again. This gave Thomas and Mary a little more time to locate the regiment as McClellan reorganized the army with his usual precision and slowness.

They arrived in the capital by the second week of September 1862. The moment they stepped off the train they could tell that something was wrong. The town was chaotic. People were hurrying everywhere and talking quickly and anxiously. Carriages sped down the dirt streets and horses raced by so fast that it became dangerous to even cross the street.

"What's going on?" Thomas asked a stranger who hurried past him in the opposite direction. The man completely ignored Thomas and continued on his way.

"What's going on?" Thomas repeated to two or three more passersby. But they too hurried past. Finally, Thomas grabbed an older man by the sleeve and held on to him as tightly as he could.

"Excuse me, sir," Thomas said as politely as possible. "What is going on? Why is the city so crazy?"

The man looked down at Thomas' hand on his sleeve. He glared at Thomas.

"I would think a soldier would know the answer to that," he said angrily.

"I...uh...I," Thomas stuttered. "I've been on leave. I just got back."

"Well, you'd better get to your unit quickly," the man snapped as he pulled his sleeve from Thomas' grasp. "General Lee's taken his army north into Maryland. It's an invasion."

Thomas' arm fell to his side and he took a step back.

"An invasion?" he repeated under his breath. "An invasion?"

Mary stopped another passerby.

"Excuse me, sir," she said politely. "Is it true that General Lee has invaded the North?"

"It sure is, young lady," the man replied. He seemed a little more friendly and a little less in a hurry. "People are saying that he wants to show the North that they don't have a chance. He even hopes to get England and France to join in."

"England and France?" Mary repeated.

"Yup," he said simply. "They have stayed out of it so far either because of our blockade or because of the South's slavery system. But lots of people think that if Lee has a good victory then they will join the war on the South's side."

"My Lord," Thomas gasped, "that would be a disaster."

"Sure would," the man agreed. "We wouldn't stand a chance then."

"W-where is he now?" Thomas managed to ask.

"Don't really know," he replied. "Some say that he's in the northwestern part of the state and headed to Pennsylvania."

"Pennsylvania?" Mary gasped. "That's my home!"

"Well, maybe you should get back there, little lady," the man said finally as he began to walk away. "And you should get to your unit, soldier."

Thomas and Mary stood staring at each other in shock. What would they do now?

"I-I've got to find my unit," Thomas finally spoke. "I've got to help."

"I'll go with you," Mary added.

"O.K.," Thomas answered. His mind was already racing as he was trying to figure out what to do next. Mary would certainly be a help in locating his unit, so it was no big deal that she was still tagging along. He'd ditch her as soon as they got close.

"Let's try the War Department," Thomas suggested.

Thomas and Mary made their way to the War Department as quickly as possible. They still were in shock at what they had heard and mumbled back and forth to each other. They had never even considered the fact that the North might lose. Ever since the war began, the North had every advantage: more men, more machines, more railroads, and even a navy. The South had nothing. How could they win?

"What if Lee makes it to Pennsylvania?" Mary wondered aloud.

"He won't," Thomas said firmly.

"How do you know?"

"I-I don't," Thomas replied.

"He hasn't lost a battle yet," Mary said after another second or two.

"I know," Thomas replied.

The War Department was in absolute chaos. Soldiers and civilians were running and yelling. It seemed as if no one knew exactly what to do or where to go. Thomas and Mary were barely able to get inside and even after they did, they only found out that the army was somewhere near the town of Frederick, Maryland.

They were able to get out of the city fairly quickly and make their way towards the Potomac. Frederick was not too far from the river, and if they got a ride upstream for awhile then they would be that much closer to the army. Mary just hoped that they would find the right army. It would not be any fun to spend the war in a Confederate prison.

. "This is as far as I can take you," the owner of the boat said after several hours. They had found a man who was willing to take his small boat up the Potomac as far as the Monocacy River but he was afraid to go any further. "You'll have to go the rest of the way on foot."

Thomas and Mary got off the boat slowly.

"Good luck finding your regiment," the man said as he pushed his boat back away from the shore.

"Thanks," Thomas said simply. "And thanks for the ride."

"No problem," the man said as he waved goodbye. "Maryland may be a border state but that doesn't mean I'm no less loyal than the rest of you. Besides," he continued as he began to row away, "if those rebels keep going, they're liable to destroy everything in the area, including my farm."

"Well, Mary," Thomas said, turning away from the river and towards his sister, "I think this is where we should say goodbye."

"So soon?" Mary complained.

"You heard the man," Thomas said. "The Confederates are all over the place. A group of 'em was in this area not more than a day or two ago."

"I know," she replied. "I just wanted to make sure that you found your unit alright."

"Don't worry about me," Thomas replied. "There are Federal units swarming in the area. I heard something about the XII Corps and the II Corps."

"You're II Corps, right?" Mary asked.

"Yeah," Thomas answered simply. "So I really should get going. Why don't you head into Frederick and talk to the local people there? They probably know where you can find a hospital unit."

"O.K.," Mary said slowly. She knew Thomas was right but she still didn't want to leave him. This might be the last time she ever saw him. "Take care of yourself, Thomas," she said finally. "You may not be a coward but you're not invulnerable either."

"Don't worry," Thomas laughed. "I'll keep my head down."

The two of them hugged. It was a long hug and Mary did not want to let go. She loved Thomas more than he ever realized. She had been his friend, his protector, his sister, and even his mother when there was no one else. Now that he was leaving to fight, she felt queasy and nervous thinking about losing him forever. She held back a tear.

"Take care of yourself, Thomas!" she called as he walked away.

Thomas stopped and looked back at his sister. "You be careful too," he replied. "Just because you don't wear a uniform doesn't mean they won't shoot you."

"I will," Mary promised. "Goodbye."

"Goodbye," Thomas replied.

Mary watched her brother walk away. "Goodbye, Thomas," she whispered one last time.[1]

---

1. To find out what happened to Thomas at the Battle of Antietam be sure to read book four of the Young Heroes of History series.

Chapter 6
Clara Barton

Mary stood at the side of the road and stared at all the activity. Wagons hurried past, and people ran down the street or rode a horse. Soldiers and townspeople screamed and yelled at each other. She had only walked into the town of Frederick a few hours ago and already had seen over ten thousand soldiers. They were everywhere, marching down the streets, stopping at stores, and taking over churches and houses to make room for prisoners or wounded. The local townspeople were overwhelmed with this sudden mass of men, animals, and equipment. They shouted orders at each other, ran down the street hauling blankets, food, or guns, or whatever else they could carry. They had a look of confusion and shock on their faces, as if they weren't sure whether this was really happening. After all, only two days ago the Confederate army had taken over the town. Now it was the Union army's turn to settle down, and it had many more soldiers.

The fighting had already begun. During the night, Mary heard the cannons firing somewhere to the west. She found out later that the Confederate and the Union men met at a place called South Mountain but she

Supply wagons heading towards the battle

wasn't sure who won. The only thing she was sure about was that there was going to be a big battle nearby. For the first time in the war, it looked as if General Lee had been caught unprepared. If General McClellan got there fast enough, he might be able to pull off a stunning upset and send Lee home with his tail between his legs. The excitement in the air was contagious and Mary could almost feel goose bumps on her arms and legs.

"What do you mean you have orders?" Mary heard a woman shouting. She turned and looked down the street to see a small, slender woman looking down angrily at several soldiers who had stopped her wagon. She had silky brown hair parted in the middle and combed into a bun at the back of her head. Her face was rather round and plain, and was matched by the plainness of her clothes. Her skirt, plain and dark, was topped by an equally plain blouse. Only the red bow at her neck gave any uniqueness to her outfit.

One of the soldiers approached the wagon to talk more with its occupants. Mary noticed two men; one sat next to the loud woman and the other man, who was probably the driver, sat in front. The wagon itself was a large covered wagon pulled by a team of six horses. The back was open and Mary could see boxes piled up inside. She wondered what they contained.

"We are to confiscate all the bread in the town for the wounded from South Mountain," the soldier replied patiently. He appeared ready for any argument the woman might give as he stood there waiting for her to comply with his request.

"The wounded from South Mountain?" the woman repeated. She seemed annoyed at his request as she

Clara Barton

thought for a moment. Mary walked towards them. She wanted to see this woman who would argue with a soldier who needed bread for the wounded.

"Yes, ma'am," the soldier replied simply.

"Well, I," the woman mumbled to herself. She looked at her two companions. They shrugged their shoulders and waited for the woman to continue. She appeared to be the one in charge.

"You ought to be ashamed of yourselves," she said finally in a disdainful tone. "You have flour, ovens, and more than enough people to make bread yourselves. What a lazy order!"

Mary watched in amazement as the two soldiers took a step back. They never had any civilian refuse a request like this before!

"My bread is for the fainting men in the field," she continued angrily, "and you shall have none of it!"

The soldiers stared awkwardly at each other. Neither one knew how to react. Mary looked at the woman's companions. They too seemed unsure what to do. Only this amazing woman seemed to be in command.

"Off with you and your lazy order!" she said one last time. "And tell your commander not to be wasting valuable resources and sending his men on errands when they could be putting their labors to better use!"

The soldiers looked at each other with a hint of embarrassment and shrugged. Then, without another word, they turned and walked away. Once they were gone, the woman sat back down in her seat on the wagon and smiled.

"Let's move on," she said to the driver.

"Wait, wait!" Mary called excitedly. She waved her hands and motioned for the wagon to halt.

"What is it now?" the woman cried.

"Please, ma'am," Mary began. She wasn't sure why she stopped this woman or what she was going to say. She just felt a need to learn more about her. She'd never seen a woman take such a tone with a man before, especially a soldier. Maybe this was someone who could help her get involved with the war. "Are you with the Sanitary Commission?"

"And who might you be, young lady?" the man next to the lady asked in a stern voice. He almost seemed like he was protecting the woman, as if she had better things to do than answer the questions of a young girl.

"M-my name is Mary Adams," Mary replied softly. She was so nervous her knees were shaking but she managed to hide it. "I am part of the soldier's aid society of Philadelphia and I've come to help."

"That's very nice of you," the man answered sincerely. His face grew softer and his voice became gentle. "But what is it you want of us?"

"I-I-I don't know," Mary said awkwardly. "I just overheard how you talked to the soldiers, ma'am," Mary directed her voice towards the woman who turned to look at her, "and I just had to meet you. After all, someone who talks to soldiers like you do would be sure to know how to help me."

"Help you do what, my dear?" the woman finally spoke. She stilled seemed impatient but at least she was taking the time to talk to Mary.

"Why, help the soldiers of course," Mary answered quickly. "Isn't that why we're all here?"

"The battlefield is no place for young girls," the woman answered gruffly. She turned her head towards the driver and waved him to move on.

"But you're going!" Mary shouted, trying to halt the wagon again.

"See here, young lady," the man scolded Mary. "This fine woman is Clara Barton, not just some stray lady rushing to the field. She has orders from Colonel Rucker himself which allow her to bring supplies to the battlefield under no command except her own."

"You're on your own?" Mary cried in disbelief. She couldn't believe that a woman would be allowed to work unsupervised. Everywhere she went, women had to work under the authority of a male supervisor whether they were a nurse, a sanitary worker, or a maid.

"That is correct," the man answered.

"Oh please, ma'am," Mary begged, "please let me come with you. No one here has let me do much work and I only want to help."

"Absolutely not," Miss Barton replied. Her voice was firm and her patience was gone. "The battlefield is no place for a young, unescorted female. I appreciate your enthusiasm and dedication, young lady. Indeed, you remind me of myself. But a young girl like you would only be seen as a loose woman, ill-mannered and improper. Now, go see if you can help in one of the hospitals that are being set up. We must move on. The battle is imminent."

She waved her hand and the wagon began moving again.

Mary stood quietly in the street and watched the wagon pull away. It wasn't fair. She wanted to help so badly. Why wouldn't anybody let her? She looked around at all the chaos in the streets. How would she ever find someone to notice her? How could she ever make a difference with so many other people around?

She turned back and looked at the wagon. It had not made it very far down the street due to all the traffic. Suddenly, an idea came to her. She looked around again to see if anyone was watching, then she ran towards the wagon.

"No one will ever notice me in all this confusion," she said to herself as she jumped onto the moving wagon. "And by the time they find me in here, it'll be too late to send me back."

Mary smiled to herself, tucked her body behind some boxes and made herself comfortable. Finally, she would be doing something important!

Chapter 7
The Wagon Ride

Mary's body was thrown forward as the wagon screeched to a stop. A pile of boxes next to her wobbled and almost fell. It was the second time today and Mary was beginning to wonder if she had made a mistake. Several hours had passed since she had jumped onto the wagon in Frederick and she was getting hungry. When the wagon had stopped a few hours ago at a church full of wounded soldiers, Mary managed to sneak out for a moment to go to the bathroom but she didn't have time to find any food. She was tempted to take food from some of the boxes in the wagon but she felt too strongly about saving it for the soldiers on the field.

Her back ached too. She didn't dare move around much for fear of being discovered. It wasn't that she was afraid they would hear her. The horses' hooves clomping on the dirt and the large wooden wheels spinning slowly along the National Road made too much noise for that. But she still was afraid of moving because the boxes were packed together tightly. One false move by Mary and they would come crashing down all around her.

"Ohhh," she moaned as she rubbed the small of her back with her left fist and squeezed her rumbling tummy with her right.

"Get down, Welles," Mary heard Miss Barton command after the wagon had completely stopped. "Let's see if we can find anyone alive in this horror."

Mary listened as Miss Barton and her companion walked around the wagon and into the field. *They're going somewhere,* she thought to herself. *Maybe I'll have a chance to find some food.*

Mary slowly moved her body around the boxes and made her way to the back of the wagon. Her muscles were achy and sore and she had trouble controlling them because they were so stiff.

"My Lord," she said out loud as she peered out the back. "What is this place?"

Mary looked around the field in disgust. It was the first time she had seen a battlefield. Immediately, her hunger vanished and was replaced by a sickening feeling in her stomach. She held her hand over her mouth and tried not to gag.

Bodies lay everywhere—not just human bodies, but horses too. Some of the dead were missing arms or legs or even heads. They were a mangled mass, stiffened and black as they rotted in the afternoon sun. Some of them lay on top of others, and in many places there were so many corpses that there was no clear path around them. Mary shivered as she realized that those bumps she had felt in the road must have been the wagon rolling over the dead bodies.

The soldiers' belongings lay scattered among the bodies as well; muskets, bayonets, knapsacks, canteens, broken wheels, and cannon balls covered the field.

Amidst this chaos stood Miss Barton and her companion, Mr. Welles. They were walking among the dead, poking and prodding them with their feet to see if anyone was still alive. It was not the sight Mary expected to see. When she had dreamed of helping on the battlefield, she imagined taking care of the living, not walking among the dead. She turned her head and looked away. Her hunger was gone.

After a short while, Miss Barton and Mr. Welles made their way back to the wagon. Except for the small number of local gravediggers, they had found no one on the field still alive.

"At least the ambulances are finally doing their jobs," Mr. Welles said to Miss Barton as he helped her back on the wagon. "It's not like it was before at Culpeper with wounded men dying in the field."

"Yes," Miss Barton agreed, motioning the driver to continue. "All the wounded seem to have been removed. We can at least be thankful that the army's ambulances are finally doing their job and saving those who can be saved."[1]

The wagon ride continued and Mary drifted in and out of sleep. Her body was weak and tired from lack of food but the ride was too bumpy for her to stay asleep for any period of time. She was also nervous. Now that she had finally made it to the front she was having doubts about whether she would have the courage to do what needed to be done. She began to wonder how she would react when she saw wounded men and men who had amputated limbs. Of course she had seen blood before. She had been bandaging up Thomas and

---

1. This was the first time that the Union army had effectively used ambulances after more than one year of war.

his dog every time they came back from a fight or a rough day on the farm. But this was different. These wounds would be gruesome. Arms and legs would be dangling from tendons, flesh would be severed and burnt, and stomachs would be opened to the air. Mary almost gagged as the images flooded her mind. How could she do this? Was she out of her mind?

The sounds outside didn't help her calm down. Cannons could be heard somewhere off to the South. Soldiers who had been wounded or left the battlefield were walking alongside the road and described the battle they had just been in. Miss Barton asked them questions about what unit they were in and where they were going. With each answer Mary became more and more upset. What could she do? It was too late to run now!

Supply wagons and convoys blocked the road for most of the evening. Something really big was about to happen. Mary held her hands tight and tried to stay calm. *Remember,* she told herself, *this is what you wanted to do. You wanted to make a difference.*

The next day brought more of the same. Fortunately, Mary was able to get some food during the night when they stopped. She was almost left behind though when Miss Barton suddenly woke up her helpers and they sped off shortly after midnight.

"This is the only way we can get around all these supply wagons," Miss Barton had said to her companions.

Throughout the morning and into the afternoon the wagon continued to speed along the road. As it got closer and closer to the front lines Mary became more agitated. *What if they send me back?* she wondered, *and make me find my way home in the middle of the battle? What if I get shot or catch one of those sicknesses that so many of the soldiers are dying from?*

She managed to make her way to the back of the wagon and peer outside. She realized that they were nearing the front lines as all the other supply wagons disappeared. The roads were instead clogged with horse-drawn artillery and companies of men. Everywhere she looked she saw the campfires of countless Union soldiers.

My Lord, Mary thought to herself, *I never imagined there would be so many people here.*

By dusk it became clear that no battle would take place that day. Although the Confederate army was within easy striking distance, General McClellan would wait one more day before he attacked. Even though, there was an "impending sense of doom"[2] hanging over everyone. The soldiers were quiet and subdued. No one played or joked around. The air was still. It was only a matter of time.

Miss Barton and her crew stopped the wagon and prepared for the night. If there was to be a battle tomorrow, they needed their rest.

Mary listened to the activity outside the wagon.

"You don't look well, Clara," she heard Mr. Welles say.

"I'm fine," Miss Barton responded quickly.

"You look pale," he commented.

"You certainly do, ma'am," the driver added.

"I'm fine, I'm fine," she insisted, "just a little drained from the ride is all."

---

2. This is how Clara Barton herself described that evening in notes she wrote later. Taken from *A Woman of Valor* by Stephen B. Oates, p. 82.

Her companions gave her looks that showed they didn't quite believe her.

"Maybe you ought to lie down," Mr. Welles suggested.

"Let me help you finish," she demanded.

"We'll do fine without you," Welles quickly replied, grabbing Miss Barton gently by the arm and leading her to the back of the wagon. "You just get some rest here in the wagon. It looks like rain soon and we can't have you collapsing from fever. We have a big day tomorrow."

"Oh no!" Mary thought in a panic, "She's headed in here! What do I do?"

"But-but," Miss Barton was protesting.

"Come on now," Welles pleaded, "I don't want to have to get rough with you," he said with a smile.

"Alright, alright," Miss Barton finally agreed with a smile on her face as well. "And thank you, Cornelius," she added as she stepped up into the back of the wagon.

Mary shrunk back as far behind the boxes as she could. What would she do now?

Chapter 8

Tears

The boxes shifted and one almost fell. Mary could hear Miss Barton grunting as she moved around, trying to get comfortable.

"I don't remember these boxes being here," Mary heard her say. "And I could have sworn there was a space over there."

Mary's heart began to pound. She wanted to scream. She wanted to run. She ducked down even more and turned her head to the side even though she knew it would do no good.

"Oww!" Miss Barton shouted as a box fell on her. "What is going on here?"

"Everything all right, Clara?" Mr. Welles called from somewhere in the field.

"Yes, yes," Miss Barton shouted in reply. "I'm just having some trouble getting comfortable."

"Do you need me to come help you?" Mr. Welles called again. He sounded as if he was in the middle of doing something.

"No, no," Miss Barton replied, "I'm fine. I just need to..."

Her voice trailed off. She stopped moving around. Mary couldn't tell where she was. All she could hear was the noises outside. Had Miss Barton finally lain down to sleep?

"Got you!" a voice shouted at the same time as a hand grabbed Mary's wrist.

"Ohh!" Mary gasped as she looked up to see Miss Barton standing over her. She had a furious look on her face and her cheeks were all red.

Both women were silent for an instant as they stared at one another and tried to figure out what to say next.

"Who are you?" Miss Barton demanded, still holding on tight to Mary's wrist.

"Please, please, Miss Barton," Mary begged. "Don't be mad. I just wanted so bad to help out."

"Help out?" Miss Barton repeated. She stared at Mary's face. "Help out?" she repeated again. "You're the girl from Frederick! The one who asked me to let her help."

"Yes," Mary answered softly. There was a sound of apology in her voice. "I was just so disappointed that you would not let me help that, I don't know, I just acted crazy. Everyone I met kept telling me to go home or that women didn't do that kind of thing. When you appeared on that road in town and started telling the soldier what to do, I knew that you were someone different. I knew that you could help me get involved."

Miss Barton did not respond but her grip on Mary's hand loosened a little.

"Then when you told me to go away," Mary continued, "I didn't know what else to do."

"So you decided to hide aboard my wagon," Miss Barton finished for her.

"Y-yes," Mary answered slowly.

"Without any idea where we were going or what we were doing?" Miss Barton asked with frustration in her voice.

"I knew it had to be something important," Mary said quickly.

"It certainly is important," Miss Barton snapped back. "It's the most important work I've ever done and I can't have some young child getting in my way!"

"I won't get in your way," Mary promised. "You won't even know I'm here."

"We certainly won't," Miss Barton said firmly, "because as soon as dawn breaks, you're leaving this camp and heading back to Frederick!"

"But...," Mary began. She looked up at Miss Barton and saw the determination in her face. There was no way she would change her mind.

Mary's head dropped down onto her chest. She had failed. All that work, all that effort wasted. She felt weak and defeated. She had come so far, gotten so close, and now it was all for nothing. She began to cry.

"Stop that right now, young lady!" Miss Barton commanded.

Mary tried to stop. She took a deep breath and held back the tears for an instant but then they began to flow again. She had never felt defeat like this. There had always been a way out before. There had always been hope that somehow her life would get better. Now, there was no hope, there was no way out. And she wasn't just crying about being caught. She was crying about her rotten life, her mean aunt and cousins, her dead parents, her lonely life on the farm. It all was so awful, and now she was finally crying about all those things. Her chest heaved heavily up and down as she sobbed.

"Stop!" Miss Barton commanded.

Mary continued to cry.

"Please, please stop," Miss Barton asked with a hint of sympathy in her voice.

Mary continued to cry.

"Please," Miss Barton repeated as she finally sat down next to Mary. "I know how you feel. I understand your disappointment."

"Y-you do?" Mary managed to say as she looked up into Miss Barton's face with tears still in her eyes.

"Of course I do," Miss Barton answered. "What woman has not felt that utter despair of living in a man's world?"

Mary sniffled a little and waited for Miss Barton to continue.

"We all suffer, my dear," she went on. "All of us. Whether you are a woman content to be a domestic servant for your whole life or one of the few who have managed to rise up in man's society. We all have suffered in our way."

"I only want to help," Mary said softly.

"Of course you do," Miss Barton said gently. She took Mary's hand in hers. "We all do. But there are proper ways and improper ways to help. There are rules that must be followed."

"You don't seem to be following any rules," Mary observed.

"I have been following the rules longer than I ever care to admit," Miss Barton said angrily. "Ever since this war began and before, I have patiently done what is expected of me. I have gathered supplies to help our soldiers and waited for permission to give them out. I have met with countless officers, many of them either too heartless or incompetent to realize the problems in the camps."

Mary had stopped crying now and was listening with interest.

"I have petitioned governors and met with leaders, both male and female, across the country and still I had to wait for permission to help."

"Why wouldn't they let you help?" Mary wondered even though she could guess the answer.

"Because I am a woman," Miss Barton said angrily, "and a woman does not belong in the army."

"How come you didn't become a nurse?" Mary asked.

"A nurse?" Miss Barton repeated with almost a chuckle. "And work for Dorothea Dix? There is no way I could work under such strict guidelines and control. I need to have some amount of independence."

Mary nodded her head in understanding. She had heard of "Dragon Dix" and her strict rules regarding nurses. They all had to be over thirty years old and meet the prim and proper guidelines she set. She didn't want any woman to be attractive or friendly to any of the soldiers for fear that they might cause an incident. It seemed absurd but Mary agreed somewhat with her desire to keep the nurses corps "respectable." Unfortunately, there were so many women who were turned away who honestly wanted to help, women like Clara Barton.

"I understand," Mary said.

There was an awkward silence.

"Well," Miss Barton said with a gasp and a clap on her knees. She rose up and looked down at Mary. "We had better get some sleep. You have a long walk ahead of you and I have important work to be ready for."

Mary hung her head in depression as Miss Barton moved to another part of the wagon to lie down. She really had lost. It was over.

Chapter 9
Something in Common

Mary heard a noise. She stirred a little and lifted her head. She wasn't sure if she had slept or if much time had passed.

She heard the noise again. It sounded like groaning.

Mary sat up and listened carefully. She could hear the rain falling on the wagon and the wind blowing outside. She could hear a footstep here and there from the soldiers on guard. Other than that it was strangely quiet, almost eerie.

Another groan. Mary turned. It was Miss Barton!

Mary moved through the wagon as quickly as she could but it was difficult in the dark. She crawled over boxes and tried to see ahead of herself by holding her hands out in front of her. She almost toppled over. She heard one more groan before she finally felt the softness of Miss Barton's blouse.

"Miss Barton, Miss Barton!" Mary called as she shook the woman gently.

"Uhhh," Miss Barton moaned.

"Miss Barton!" Mary repeated. "Are you alright?"

"Mm, mm," she mumbled. "Cornelius?"

"It's Mary," she reminded her. "You were moaning in your sleep and you sounded like you were in pain."

"Mary?" she said as she began to rise. "Mmm, oh yes. The girl who stowed away. What is it, child?"

"You were moaning in your sleep and you sounded like you were in pain," Mary repeated.

"Oh, well, yes, thank you," Miss Barton said as she rubbed her face with her hands and tried to straighten herself out. "I was having a terrible nightmare. It must be the fever."

"Fever?"

"It's nothing to worry about," Miss Barton said quickly. She didn't want anyone to know she was sick. She didn't even want to admit it to herself. She had too much important work to do.

"Are you sick?" Mary asked.

"No, no, child," Miss Barton replied quickly with a wave of her hand. "Now go back to sleep. You have a long walk ahead of you."

"I'm not tired," Mary said quickly. She had no desire to spend her last hours with Miss Barton sleeping in a corner.

Miss Barton sat quietly. She rubbed her face and looked around. She blinked several times and then yawned.

"What was your nightmare about?" Mary dared to ask.

"It was nothing, really."

"It must have been bad the way you were moaning," Mary reminded her.

"Was I really moaning?" Miss Barton asked.

"Oh yes," Mary replied emphatically. "I was really worried."

"Well, you don't need to be," Miss Barton assured her. "I'm fine. But thank you for your concern."

"You're welcome."

Both women were quiet again. Mary struggled to think of something to say.

"It really was a terrible dream." Miss Barton suddenly broke the silence. Mary turned her head quickly to show her interest but did not interrupt.

"My mother and father were both there," Miss Barton explained, "but they didn't seem to care where I was. And my brother Stephen was there as well but he was unable to speak, as if someone had cut out his tongue."

"Oh my," Mary said.

"But that wasn't the worst part," she went on. "Soldiers were there too, both grey and blue. They weren't fighting though, they were slowly dying and I tried to help them but my mother wouldn't let me. She kept hitting me and calling me names."

"What did your father do?"

"He was trying to help me but for some reason he couldn't."

Miss Barton thought for a moment.

"He was dying," she realized. "Dying slowly, just like he did in real life."

"You lost your father?" Mary asked.

"And my mother," Miss Barton added.

"Me too," Mary said sadly.

Miss Barton turned her head and looked at Mary. For the first time she saw Mary as the confused and frightened girl that she was. She began to understand Mary a lot more now that she took the time to talk to her.

The rain continued to fall. It had a soothing, gentle feeling that calmed Miss Barton. She wasn't angry anymore. In fact, she felt depressed and guilty. Mary was so much like her. Inside, they were both little girls who had been hurt and were now alone in an unfriendly world. They both had lost their parents. They both had taken that empty feeling and attempted to replace it with a love of helping others. And now each of them had a burning desire to find a way to comfort the soldiers, yet all anyone could do was tell them to go away. Then, as if a mirror had suddenly been thrown in front of her, Miss Barton realized that she had been treating Mary the same way that she had been treated by so many others. She had become so concerned with her desire to get to the front lines that she completely ignored Mary's feelings.

A huge explosion shattered the silence. Both women jumped at the sound.

"What was that?" Mary cried.

"I don't know," Miss Barton answered. "But I'd better go find out. You stay here."

"But...," Mary protested as Miss Barton scrambled up and out of the wagon.

It seemed as if Miss Barton was gone for hours. Mary could hear the explosions far off and imagined Miss Barton standing up on the hill looking for the signs of battle.

"I hope she is alright," Mary thought to herself.

The explosions grew louder and seemed to be coming from all around. The wagon shook as the concussions ripped through the air. Mary had to hold her ears to muffle the deafening blasts. It sounded as if the ground itself was ripping up to destroy them.

"Cornelius, Cornelius!" Mary heard Miss Barton shout over the noise.

"Over here, Clara!" Mr. Welles called back. "We're ready!"

"It's begun!" Miss Barton declared as she neared the wagon.

Mr. Welles and the driver looked at Miss Barton with grim faces. This was what they had prepared for. They prayed that they were ready.

"Let's go!" Miss Barton commanded.

Mary felt the wagon lurch forward. In all of the confusion, Miss Barton either forgot about her or didn't care. Mary smiled. She would get to the front lines after all.

Chapter 10
The Front Lines

Mary waited nervously. The wagon had been moving for several hours as Miss Barton's team searched for a place where they were needed the most. All Mary could do was listen to the horrible sounds of battle and the voices of the soldiers who stopped to talk to Miss Barton. From their comments, she could tell that it was a terrible fight.

Even hidden inside the wagon and surrounded by boxes, Mary could feel the concussions of the cannon explosions. She could hear the gunfire and the screams of the men as they fought for their lives. She imagined all of the soldiers who were lying in pain and slowly dying. This was going to be the hardest thing she had ever done in her life. She prayed that she would be ready.

Mary's stomach growled. In all of the confusion she realized she had not eaten. The sun had been up for a while and she was beginning to feel weak. *Gather your strength,* she told herself. *You're going to need it.*

Swishing, banging noises could be heard outside. It sounded as if thousands of whips were snapping or brushing up against the wagon. Mary snuck a peak through the back and saw tall cornstalks being pushed to the side as the wagon made its way through a cornfield.

"Here is where we are needed," Mary heard Miss Barton say to her companions.

The wagon stopped. The driver and Mr. Welles jumped off the wagon and began to unhitch the mules.

"Unload the supplies!" Miss Barton commanded.

"Oh my," Mary thought to herself. "This is it! They're going to find me."

Mary could see hands grasping supply boxes as one by one they were taken out of the wagon and laid on the ground nearby.

"Quickly, quickly!" Mary could hear Miss Barton shouting over the gunfire and screams.

We must be really close, Mary realized.

"What the?..." the driver shouted as he pulled away a box to reveal Mary sitting there.

"Hi," she said with a wave of her hand.

"Mary!" Miss Barton cried as she spun around. "I'd completely forgotten about you."

"You knew about this stowaway?" Mr. Welles cried in disbelief.

"I discovered her last night," Miss Barton explained patiently. "And I was going to send her back this morning but obviously I got distracted."

"What are we going to do with her?" the driver wondered. He had stopped unloading the supplies as he listened to Miss Barton.

"What can we do?" Miss Barton asked. "It's too late to send her away now, and we've got work to do." She stared at the driver. Her eyes glared, as if she was expecting him to do something.

"Oh," he mumbled as he realized that she wanted him to continue unloading the wagon.

"Now listen, Mary," Miss Barton said sternly once the two men began unloading the wagon again. "You need to stay out of the way. We are in the middle of a battlefield and I don't want you getting hurt or getting in the way."

Mary's face dropped as she realized that she would not be allowed to help after all. "But...," she whined.

Miss Barton was not even there to argue. She had already turned around and made her way towards an old barn.

Mary watched as the men finished unloading the wagon and took the supplies to the barn. They didn't say a word to her and their eyes stayed cast down, as if they did not want to look at Mary.

Don't treat me like I'm not here, she thought angrily. *My aunt used to do that all the time and I hated it.*

While the men continued to carry the supplies up to the barn, Mary looked out at the cornfield. They were right on the front lines. Screams could be heard from just beyond the trees where a battle was raging. On a hill, just past the cornfield, Mary could also see a group of Union cannons protecting a Federal infantry unit. They looked as if they were waiting for an attack.

Directly in front of Mary, lying in the cornfield and waiting by the barn was a group of wounded Union soldiers. Some men were missing a limb, others were holding their side in an attempt to prevent more bleeding, and still more had different degrees

One of the farmhouses used as a hospital during the battle

of head injuries. One man was trying desperately to keep his insides from falling out onto the bloody grass beneath him. Many of them were crying or groaning and a few looked as if they were in shock. They all were too injured to move and Mary wondered where the surgeons were to help them.

"Over here." Mary saw the driver point to Miss Barton. "There is a farmhouse over here with tables and surgeons."

As the three figures headed away from the wagon and into the cornfield, Mary watched in frustration. She had come so far. She had done so much. And now all she could do was watch. Why was she listening to this woman? Was it because she was a woman? Mary had always had a hard time saying no to her mother and aunt. Maybe it was just because they were older and she had always been taught to respect adults.

Mary set her jaw and fixed her eyes on the receding volunteers. *I'm not a kid anymore*, she told herself. *I've been taking care of my brother and sister for years now. I've taken care of cooking for the family and cleaning the house since I was little. I've worked for the soldier's aid society and I've helped my brother travel all the way here to Maryland. Why am I letting them tell me what to do? They're not my boss. They're not even in the army. They have no authority over me. They're just volunteers like I am!*

Mary jumped out of the wagon and walked towards the farm. She ignored the flying bullets and the sound of cannon balls as they whistled overhead. Trees exploded nearby and fell to the ground as they were struck by artillery shells. Mary ignored the terrifying battle sounds and focused on finding wounded men who needed help.

As she approached the farm, she could see Miss Barton talking with a man that she had never seen before. He was dressed in a military uniform and Mary guessed that he was a surgeon. He was leading Miss Barton around, showing her all of the problems and pointing to the many wounded men who were waiting to be operated on. On the porch, Mary could see four soldiers lying on tables, waiting for treatment. Nearby was a pile of arms and legs from the many amputations that had already been performed. Mary shuddered. She knew to expect this but it still was hard to look at.

"Water," a voice cried from nearby.

Mary looked down and to her left. Lying in the corn was a soldier with blood all over his stomach. His hand held a bandage over a hole in his belly but it was not doing much good. Mary knelt down to help him.

"Th-thank you," the man smiled as he lifted his head slightly to accept the canteen of water. Mary placed her hand gently under his head and lifted it further to her canteen.

"Stay still," Mary urged the man. "Help has arrived. You'll be alright."

The man let out a sigh as he finished drinking. Then his head sunk down to the ground again and he closed his eyes.

"I've done it," Mary thought to herself. "I've helped."

A sense of power and accomplishment washed over Mary. She had broken the bonds. She had made it onto the battlefield and was doing something important. She felt great.

More groans alerted Mary that there was much more to be done. She turned and made her way to the wounded men in need of aid.

"Who is that?" a voice yelled from the porch. It was the chief surgeon! He had seen Mary and was pointing angrily at her. "What is that girl doing here in the middle of a battle?"

Mary turned in shock and fright. She had forgotten that Clara Barton was not the only one who might try to stop her. This man, who truly did hold power, could easily get rid of Mary or even have her arrested.

"She is my assistant," Miss Barton said softly with a wink in Mary's direction. Obviously, Miss Barton had changed her mind. Whether it was because of how impressed she was with Mary's determination or because they really could use the help, Mary would never know. Maybe it was even that Miss Barton was embarrassed that she could not control a girl who had stowed away on her wagon. Whatever the reason, Miss Barton had decided to let Mary help. "She may look young, but believe me, she will be a help," she added.

"Well, if you vouch for her," the surgeon replied calmly, "then it's fine with me. We certainly can use any help we can get."

Mary let out a huge sigh of relief and smiled at Miss Barton. "Thank you," she mouthed.

With the permission to help out however she could, Mary set to work with an intensity that was matched only by Miss Barton herself. Mr. Welles, other surgeons, and the dozen or so soldiers who volunteered their aid were amazed by the energy that Mary and Miss Barton had. With wounded men lying everywhere, the women patiently went from man to man, comforting them, applying bandages, giving them water, or simply talking to them to calm their nerves.

Bullets flew everywhere. Cannon shells burst overhead, in the nearby trees, and even among the wounded. Miss Barton even had a bullet penetrate her dress and strike the chest of a man she was tending to! The bullets struck the farmhouse so often that holes were in the floors, the walls, and even the ceiling.

The wounded arrived faster than they could be handled. From what Mary could find out, it was a terrible, costly battle. Thousands of men were being cut down in their tracks. Mary talked to several soldiers who lamented that their entire regiment, officers and all, had been destroyed. For every wounded soldier that Mary consoled, she realized that there was another man lying in the grass on the battlefield who would never move again. The thought only made her more determined to save whomever she could.

She realized that what she was doing was important. She wasn't just giving the men a shoulder to cry on. She was cleaning their wounds or comforting them enough so they could endure amputation or giving them enough water or food so that they could stay alive until treatment arrived.

She found a soldier lying on the ground waiting for an amputation. He had been shot in the leg just below his kneecap. Mary managed to stop the bleeding, but she knew that if the leg was not cut off it would eventually turn green and the infection spread to the rest of his body.

"Please, please, don't let them cut me!" the soldier cried, tugging at Mary's dress while she wiped his forehead. "I don't want to lose my leg!"

"It's O.K., it's O.K.," Mary said soothingly, trying to calm the panicking soldier. She could tell that he wasn't much older than she was. His face still had that youthful softness and he didn't have the unshaven look that many of the older soldiers had. She noticed he even had a pimple or two on his nose.

"No, no, no!" he screamed, still tugging and pulling at Mary's dress. Despite his wound, he was quite strong and his panic only made him stronger. "Don't let them do it! Don't let them do it!"

He pulled Mary down onto his chest, still screaming at her. She tried to wriggle free but was unable. Then, she looked into his eyes. His senses must have left him completely in the realization that he would soon have his leg sawed in half. All Mary could see was a desperate fear, almost a panic, as his eyes darted back and forth. She thought about what was going to happen to this soldier and she wondered how she would act if her leg was about to be cut off.

"Please, please," Mary begged, trying to push herself free, "let me go."

"Don't let them do it!" the soldier continued screaming. His arms were wrapped tight around Mary's back and his fingernails dug into her skin. "I can't bear the pain! I can't! I can't! I can't!"

Mary reached out and grabbed the man's right arm. With all of her strength she flung it forward and pulled herself back a little. She took a deep breath and looked the man straight in the eyes.

"Don't worry," she said softly and firmly. Her hand grabbed his chin and she forced the soldier to look at her. His eyes were still ablaze with horror but at least he was listening. "We have all the chloroform we need.

You won't feel a thing. When you wake up it will all be over and your life will have been saved."

"C-c-chloroform?" he repeated slowly. He calmed down a bit and seemed to be listening.

"Yes, chloroform," Mary repeated quickly, trying to keep his attention. "It will put you to sleep before a surgeon ever touches you."

The soldier stopped tugging at Mary but he still held her close. "I had heard that everyone had run out," he said in confusion.

"Everyone else has," Mary answered. "But not us. Miss Barton has gathered supplies from all over the country and we still have plenty."

Mary was not telling the complete truth. Although they still had some supplies left, even they were running low. With all of the wounded coming in, Mary knew that they would eventually have to perform operations without chloroform as the other stations had started to already. Then, the only thing that would comfort the soldiers while their arm or leg was being sawn off was some whisky.

"Miss Barton?" the soldier wondered.

"Yes," Mary replied, finally being able to sit up, now that the soldier had calmed down. "She is a wonderful woman who has dedicated her life to helping soldiers just like you."

"Whew!" the soldier whistled.

"Now get some rest," Mary commanded. "You're going to need it." She held the soldier's hand for a moment and squeezed tight. He squeezed back and gave a small smile.

"Thank you," he said softly.

Mary smiled. "You're welcome," she responded as she stood up and looked for another soldier who needed her help.

Things really were getting desperate, Mary realized. It was still only early afternoon and the line of wounded stretched out hundreds of feet past the farm. Food was running low. How would they ever have enough supplies or people to tend to so many men?

Mary pressed on. She bandaged wounds. She poured water. She comforted men and cleaned their faces. Her hands had gashes from the constant cutting she was doing. Her face was blackened from the powder and ash in the air. Her ears rang from the constant shelling. Her back ached from bending over soldier after soldier. And yet, she pressed on.

Although the fighting died down in the immediate area of the farm, things did not get any better. Fighting further up the lines actually intensified and most of the surgeons were called away. Mary found herself cleaning more wounds and even cutting rotted flesh from around bullet holes. Mr. Welles was forced to take over for the absent surgeons and had to extract a bullet from a young soldier's leg.

At four o'clock in the afternoon it got worse. Rebel artillery fired at the Union cannon nearby. Shells exploded overhead and in the cornfield around the farm. The Union cannon responded and a duel began around the field, with Mary caught right in the middle. The house shook as each shock wave smashed into the walls with a deafening roar. Mary could not hear herself shouting and she covered her ears for fear that she would go deaf. Smoke filled the room and became so dense that it was difficult to see. The sulphur from the gunpowder hung in the air, scorched Mary's lungs, and dried her lips so much that they almost bled.

The tables bounced around the floor. Wounded men screamed as they were jolted back and forth. A surgeon conducting an operation found himself all alone as the male nurses ran for cover. Mary saw him shouting something. Then Miss Barton approached and Mary watched as she steadied the table and helped the surgeon finish the operation. Mary marveled at the sight of Miss Barton standing firm in this chaos while all of the men ran away.

Fortunately, the terrible cannon battle did not last very long. Afterwards, a strange quiet was present as the battle shifted down the field. With a sigh of relief, Mary continued her work.

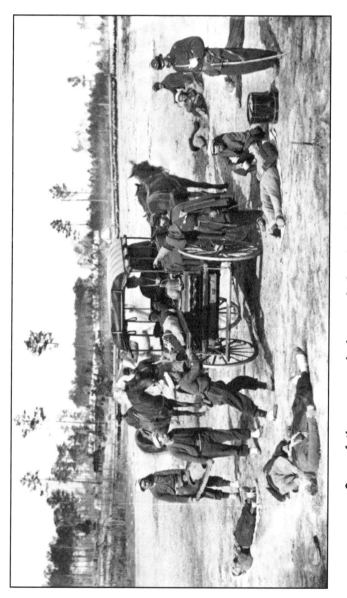

One of the new ambulances being loaded with wounded

Chapter 11
The Next Day

The work continued throughout the rest of the day and into the night. At one point the chief surgeon despaired that he had no way of working in the dark. His candles were almost all burnt out. Then Miss Barton showed him the lanterns she had brought with her.

"You truly are an angel," he said to her in gratitude.

Of course many of the men would not live to see the next day. Mary spent much of her time feeding them, comforting them, and talking with those who felt they would not survive. It gave Mary a strange mix of emotions. She was overwhelmed with grief and pain as she stared into the eyes of these young men and boys who were about to die. Yet she also felt a sense of pride and accomplishment because at least she was there to help ease their pain or listen to their last thoughts. She never thought she'd be a priest as well as a nurse.

At dawn, Mary joined Miss Barton and Mr. Welles outside. They walked to the battlefield.

"What is this place?" Mary wondered aloud as they left the barn. She realized that in all the excitement and confusion she never found out where she was.

"We are near the Maryland town of Sharpsburg," Mr. Welles responded, "near Antietam Creek. These farmhouses are on the outskirts of the town and these cornfields..."

Mr. Welles' voice trailed off and he abruptly stopped walking. They had reached the battlefield.

"This is horrible," Miss Barton gasped as she stood at the edge of the bloody cornfield. Under the bright blue sky, with the trees swaying in the wind and amidst the shattered buildings, trampled cornstalks, and broken equipment were thousands of dead soldiers. Their bodies lay everywhere, in all manner of positions. Union and rebel corpses rotted and bloated in the sun as flies swarmed around. In some cases, heads, arms, and legs lay apart from the mangled bodies. Even dead horses were lying throughout the field. The smell and the sights made Mary gag. She turned away.

"My God," she cried as tears began to swell up in her eyes. "I never imagined, I never dreamed..."

"No one can," Mr. Welles said softly as he placed a hand on Mary's shoulder. "No one can ever imagine the terror we inflict upon ourselves."

"If only the politicians and hotheads in the government could see this," Miss Barton added.

"How," Mary gasped, still trying to steady herself, "how can we do this? How can we destroy so much life, cause so much pain?"

No one responded. After all, what could be said? How could anyone explain such senseless destruction and loss of human life? All of these men were sons or fathers or brothers. All of them left loved ones back home to fight for what they believed in. Who would explain their loss to the families? Who would comfort the orphaned child or the widow or the mother?

Why are we doing this? Mary thought to herself. *Why are we destroying so much life? Is it just to keep a country together? Does the United States of America really mean so much to us that we would do this? Does independence and freedom mean so much to the Southerners that they would destroy us all?*

"Their deaths have to mean something!" Mary suddenly blurted out. "We can't let all these people die for nothing."

"They won't," Miss Barton said sternly. There was clear determination in her voice. "They won't. We will win this war. We will see to it that the United States of America is made whole again."

"Is that all?" Mary shot back. Her anger surprised everyone including herself. "Only to keep the country together? All these people will have died just so that we could have one country instead of two?"

"That is no small accomplishment," Mr. Welles responded angrily. He did not like what Mary was implying. He loved his country and was proud of what he was doing to help the war effort. "The United States of America is the only true democracy in the world. We are the last hope of oppressed people, the only country on the planet which is not ruled by a king."

"We are also the only ones on the planet with such a vile system of slavery," Mary quipped. She had found her strength now. She had found her answer to her own question. She stood up strong and stared at Mr. Welles and Miss Barton.

"You are right," Miss Barton conceded. "You are absolutely right and maybe after this war is over, that miserable evil will be as dead as the men on this field."

"It can't be maybe," Mary replied. Her determination surprised Miss Barton. She thought Mary was here to help the soldiers and that was all. She had no idea that Mary was such a strong abolitionist. "We must free the slaves. We must make all this suffering and death mean more than just Union and country."

"And how do we do that?" Mr. Welles wondered. He knew the answer and understood all the politics behind the problem but he still wanted to hear how Mary felt about it.

"We must make the president and the other politicians realize what this fight is for," Mary replied. "We must get him to free the slaves, to turn this into a war to end slavery and not just a war to keep the country together."

"He won't do that," Mr. Welles answered. "He doesn't dare. The border states still have slaves and they would join the rebellion as well if he outlawed slavery."

"Then let them!" Mary almost yelled. "Let them leave the Union and they too will suffer the same fate."

"And spread this suffering even more?" Miss Barton scolded as she swept her arm over the battlefield. "You talk nobly, child, but there is no wisdom behind your words."

Mary shrunk back. She hadn't meant to offend.

"It is not as easy as simply declaring the slaves free," Miss Barton went on. "There are so many other considerations, so many other problems to solve."

Miss Barton looked over the field again and sighed.

"And we have our own problems to deal with," she said finally. "We can't spend any more time discussing politics when there are more wounded to take care of. Come Cornelius," she said affectionately as she turned away, "let's get back to work."

Mary stood for a moment as the two companions wandered off.

"Wait!" she cried. "What about me?"

"You have done your part," Miss Barton said as she stopped to talk with Mary. "You have performed far better than any other woman or man I have ever seen. And you are to be commended for the work you have performed."

Mary looked on nervously, waiting for her to continue.

"But it is time for us to take our leave of you now," Miss Barton said with finality. "We cannot continue to have you tag along as we do our work, even though you were a great help."

A look of panic appeared in Mary's eyes but before she could even complain, Miss Barton sensed her concerns and continued, "I will give you a letter of introduction so that you will be able to find some volunteer work in Frederick or elsewhere."

Mary's head dropped but she still managed to say a mumbled "Thank You."

"And after the battle," Miss Barton continued, trying to lift Mary's spirits, "you can use the letter to get more involved in the aid societies in Philadelphia. Some of their representatives may even be here shortly, so you should keep an eye out for them."

"Representatives?" Mary repeated.

"Yes," Mr. Welles answered patiently. He felt sorry for Mary as well and he may have even wished she could come but he knew it would be impossible. "Many of the soldier's aid societies send representatives to the field to make sure their supplies are distributed properly. I am sure that there will eventually be someone from

Philadelphia here since they are a major supplier. You are from Philadelphia, aren't you?"

"Just outside," Mary informed him.

"Then it should be easy for you to find work in the war effort," Mr. Welles said with a smile.

"Come, Cornelius," Miss Barton urged. "The battle may begin again soon."

Chapter 12

The Soldier

The battle did not begin again. General Lee did not want to continue the fight and General McClellan was unsure of his chances. The Battle of Antietam ended in a draw.

The bloodiest day in American history had come and gone. In less than twenty-four hours, over 3,500 men had been killed and more than five times that number had been wounded. Mary would have plenty of work to do.

Finding the hospitals was even easier than she thought it would be. After following the ambulances and wagons for eighteen miles, she again arrived in the nearby town of Frederick where many of the wounded were being taken. Mary then asked a few officers for directions and within an hour she found a church that needed help. Actually every church, meeting hall, and government building had been turned into a makeshift hospital. There were so many wounded crowding the streets and the buildings that the new ambulance corps was unable to transport them all to the major army hospitals in Philadelphia and Washington, D.C.

Many hospitals were converted from public buildings like this one photographed by Mathew Brady.

National Archives

Miss Barton's letter of introduction allowed Mary to work directly with the wounded. She could not be a nurse but she could help by getting food and drink for the wounded, cleaning the hospitals, or running errands. It was a crazy, chaotic, loud mess, and Mary loved it.

She was involved. She was in the center of all the action, seeing firsthand what was going on. Even when she was cleaning up dirty floors or scrubbing blood off a wall she felt important. Finally she was contributing.

Of course she was tired and hungry. She did not get much sleep, and when she did find the chance to eat, the food was usually cold and tasteless. In the beginning she did not have much of an appetite, but as she got used to the disgusting sights and smells she found that she was hungrier than ever.

One day when she had stopped for a break she noticed a wounded soldier yelling at a nurse.

"No! No!" he was screaming. "Please don't tear it. Please!"

The commotion grabbed Mary's attention. She had never seen a soldier so upset about being undressed before.

"Stop, stop!" he continued to cry.

"Can I help?" Mary said to the nurse who was still trying to cut the trousers off the soldier.

"Who are you?" the nurse barked back angrily. He was in no mood to deal with anyone while this soldier was screaming.

"No one special," Mary replied. "But I've been working with soldiers long enough to know that if you calm them down first then it is easier to get what you want."

"You think so?" he snapped. Mary could tell he had no patience for her either.

"Yes, I do," Mary responded simply. "And in fact, if you let me take over, I bet you'll be able to get your other work done sooner."

"Fine with me," the man gave in as he dropped the wounded soldier's leg and held up his hands. "He's all yours."

Mary looked down at the soldier as the nurse walked away. He had a strange look in his eyes. It was a panic Mary had never seen before and she was unsure of what to do next.

"Please, please," the soldier began, trying to sit up on the stretcher, "leave me alone. All I want to do is return to my unit."

"But you've been shot," Mary replied. "Your thigh looks shattered and the bullet is still lodged inside."

"No it's not," the soldier protested. "I cut it out myself."

"Yourself?" Mary gasped. "Why would you do a thing like that?"

"Because I don't want you to amputate it," the soldier admitted.

"We don't amputate everything," Mary said defensively. "But we may have to if you have done more damage fixing it yourself."

"It's fine," the soldier argued.

"Well, let me be the judge of that," Mary said as she reached down towards his leg.

"No!" he shouted. "Don't touch me!"

Mary took a step back. She had never encountered such hostility before. He seemed not only angry but even afraid of her.

"I just want to..."

"Don't!" he screamed. "Just leave me alone!"

Mary stared at the soldier. She couldn't understand what he was so upset about. All she wanted to do was look at the wound. Then, as she continued to stare at the soldier, she began to notice some strange things about him.

His face was soft and smooth. There was no sign at all of any facial hair and this soldier had been lying out for days. He should have some hair, even if it was only stubble. Mary looked down at his hands. They were extremely small and the fingers were skinnier than any she had seen before.

Maybe this soldier is still a boy, Mary thought to herself. *After all, my younger brother Thomas managed to sign up.*

But something else was strange about this boy. His body size was all wrong. If he was a boy who was too young to shave then why was he so big? He looked at least sixteen.

Maybe..., Mary thought. And then an idea came to her. This soldier did not want to be looked at. He did not want to be undressed. Mary stared at him again, trying to see any signs that confirmed what she was thinking.

"What's your name, soldier?" she said suddenly.

"L-larry," the soldier replied.

"Where are you from, Larry?" Mary asked.

"M-maine," he said.

"And why don't you want me to look at your leg?" Mary said quickly, trying to catch him off guard.

"I-I-I just don't," the soldier stuttered.

"Listen," Mary said softly as she sat next to him on the stretcher. She decided she would try out her theory. "You can trust me. I think I know why you don't want me to look at your leg."

"Y-you do?" the soldier said nervously. The fear in his eyes was constant now.

"Yes, I do," Mary answered boldly. "And I think you should let me look at it. After all, someone is going to eventually even if they have to tie you down."

The soldier began to shake his head violently.

"But if you let me look at it," Mary finished, "I'll be sure to keep your secret."

"W-what secret?" the soldier tried to say.

Mary gave him a look. He shrugged his shoulders.

"I know you're hiding something," Mary scolded.

"What makes you say that?" he asked innocently.

"Why else would you hide your wound from me?"

"I just don't want to, O.K.?" he snapped.

"No, it's not O.K.," Mary snapped back. "You have a terrible wound here and if it's not looked at and treated, the infection could spread to your body and you could die. Now let me look at that wound or I'll get some men in here to tie you down."

Larry looked around nervously. No one had seen them talking. Everyone seemed either too busy to care or too tired to notice. He saw a surgeon on the opposite side of the room who was looking at another soldier's leg. Sooner or later he would make his way across the room.

"You promise to keep my secret?" he asked Mary.

Mary nodded. She still wasn't sure what his secret was but it was the only way to get a look at the wound.

"O.K.," Larry finally gave in. He removed his hand from his thigh and let Mary see it.

"It's not as bad as I thought," Mary commented as she took out her scissors and began to cut Larry's pants. "You did a pretty good job."

Larry smiled awkwardly and looked down at his pants leg. He was extremely nervous and jumpy. Mary had to warn him twice to settle down otherwise she might accidently cut his leg.

Mary looked into his eyes. The fear was still there but now there was a look of hope and anticipation. He seemed to be begging her to understand and help him.

Slowly, more and more of the pants leg came off to reveal the skin and clothing underneath. Then as Mary began to see his abdomen she realized why this soldier was so afraid.

"You're a girl!" Mary gasped.

Chapter 13

Confidantes

The soldier stared at Mary. She was waiting to see what her reaction would be.

"A girl!" Mary repeated. "But, but, how, how?..." Mary mumbled.

"Private Lynn Rhodes, 7th Maine, at your service," Lynn said with a slight smile. She was relieved to finally tell someone. After all it had been over a year since she and Daniel had enlisted together. She had grown very tired of the secrecy and the pretending, of the lies and the half-truths. She had tired of the girl jokes and pretending they were funny. She had grown tired of the whole thing. If she hadn't cared so much for the boys in her unit she might have left a long time ago.

"Lynn?" Mary managed to repeat. "How did you?..."

"Join up?" Lynn finished for her. "It was easy. I just cut my hair, taped down my chest, and here I am." She smiled again. She was proud that she had been able to hide her secret for so long.

"But how did you keep it a secret?" Mary wondered aloud. She still couldn't believe what she was seeing.

"It wasn't so hard," Lynn answered. "I'm sure you realize how rarely soldiers bathe. Between that and having my twin brother in the same company, it was a cinch to fool everyone."

"Twin brother?" Mary repeated.

"Yeah," Lynn answered. "His name's Daniel Rhodes."

"But why would you want to do this?" Mary gasped. Despite what she had done to get where she was, Mary still couldn't believe that a woman would pretend to be a man. What good would it do? What would she prove?

"To get involved, of course," Lynn responded quickly. She was surprised and a little annoyed that Mary would be asking her this question. "Isn't that why you're here?"

"Y-yes but..."

"But what?" Lynn charged. "I don't belong in a uniform? I should be content taking care of the wounded and cleaning their mess?"

"This is an important job!" Mary shouted. Other soldiers lying in their beds looked up. The surgeon raised his head as well.

"Yeah, yeah, fine," Lynn whispered as she made a shushing motion with her hands. "Whatever you say. Just keep it down, O.K.?"

Mary nodded slightly. She still wasn't sure what she was going to do. Lynn had obviously broken the rules and it was only a matter of time before she was caught. But still, Mary did not want to be the one to turn Lynn in. Although she did not agree with what Lynn was doing, it was still a brave thing that Mary respected. Besides, she wasn't a snitch.

"So?" Lynn asked. She had sensed a weakness in Mary. Now she was trying to press her advantage. "Are you going to turn me in?"

Mary did not answer. Her head was spinning. She didn't want to get into trouble. She had worked too hard to get where she was to lose it all now. What would she do? Should she turn her in? For what? Being a woman? As far as she knew there wasn't any law that said a woman couldn't fight. It just wasn't done. But then again, women had never been allowed on the front lines before either. Everything seemed to be changing. The whole world was upside down.

"Ummm," Mary mumbled.

"I haven't done anything wrong," Lynn added, trying to convince Mary before she made up her mind. "I've fought for my country like any good citizen would do."

"Yeah," Mary whispered as she nodded, "you have."

"It's not my fault that men make the rules," Lynn continued.

That's for sure, Mary thought to herself. *It's certainly kept me from doing what I wanted to do. At least until I met Clara Barton.*

"Then are we O.K.?" Lynn asked hopefully, her eyes pleading with Mary.

"I-I guess so," Mary replied. "At least for now."

"Whew!" Lynn gasped as she let out a huge sigh. "Thanks, uh..."

There was an awkward pause as Lynn stared questioningly at Mary.

"Mary," she answered once she realized what Lynn wanted. "Mary Adams," she said, holding out her hand.

"Nice to meet you, Mary," Lynn smiled, returning the handshake.

"What's going on here, soldier?" a voice suddenly interrupted.

Lynn and Mary turned around to see a Union army officer towering over them. He was a huge man, at least six feet tall with large rounded shoulders and even larger hands. His face was covered in ash and gunpowder and a scar ran down his left cheek. He looked like a giant ready to gobble up his prey with a large swoop of his hand.

"N-nothing, sir," Lynn said as she saluted awkwardly and covered herself with a blanket. "I was just chatting with this woman about the battle."

"Hmmm, yes," the officer replied, glancing over at Mary for an instant. It still was not normal for a woman to be in a medical unit, even if it was a private home that had been confiscated by the army. He ignored Mary however and turned back to Lynn. "What a battle it was. What unit are you in, soldier?"

"S-Seventh Maine, sir," Lynn answered.

"7th Maine?" the officer repeated. He had a deep, burly voice and when he spoke it vibrated through Lynn's ears. A look of concern suddenly washed over him as he moved in closer to Lynn. "You got cut up pretty bad, didn't you?"

"Y-yes, sir," Lynn replied as the memories of that day came rushing back to her. She backed up a little and ruffled her blanket as the officer got closer. She certainly didn't want him to see her. "It was horrible."

"Caught in a crossfire, weren't you?"

"Ambushed is more like it," Lynn explained.

The officer raised his eyebrow, waiting for Lynn to continue.

"We had been ordered in by Colonel Irwin," Lynn began. She stared straight ahead as the memories took over. "There wasn't much action at first. The skirmishers pushed the rebs ahead in our path. Then I heard the order to fix bayonets and we charged ahead. There was some fire and a few men fell but it was nothing we hadn't seen before."

Mary turned and looked at Lynn. She really had been a soldier! And this wasn't her first time. She was talking as if she had seen many battles. *She must have seen an awful lot,* Mary realized.

"The reb lines broke," Lynn went on, "and we were thinking that all was going well when suddenly a reb regiment rose up from behind a stone wall on our right and began pouring it on. They double-quicked to our right and cut off our retreat and before we knew it we were surrounded."

The officer sat down on Lynn's cot, never taking his eyes off her. He and Mary were spellbound, waiting to hear what happened next.

"They were firing on us from three directions," Lynn spoke quickly. She sounded as if she were really there. Her voice was edgy and her eyes darted back and forth. She began to sweat. "Then artillery opened up on us. It was a terrible mass of confusion. I noticed at least four different reb battle flags. I wasn't sure which way to fire. Men were screaming and dying all around me. I felt a sharp pain in my leg and a sudden thud. I staggered a little and my brother grabbed my shoulder to steady me. He yelled at me to hold on because he knew that we were about to get overrun."

Lynn's eyes were totally glazed over now as she completely relived the event. Her voice ran on as she poured out the story to Mary and the officer.

"Our ammunition began to run out. My leg was burning like it was on fire. Everyone was going down. I saw Lieutenant Brown and Shorey go down. And then Captain Jones went down and Captain Cochrane and more enlisted men. I saw our flag go down. I thought for sure that this was it, that I would die right there."

Lynn stopped for a second and took a deep breath. She shuddered. She took another breath and gasped. Mary and the officer waited patiently. Then, as Mary stared at Lynn, she felt a sudden sense of shock. Under Lynn's right eye, just to the side of her nose was a tear slowly flowing down her face.

Mary turned and looked quickly at the officer. Had he noticed? What would he do if he did? Mary had seen other soldiers cry before and it was not totally uncommon but maybe this officer had never seen it. Maybe he would think that Lynn was a weakling. Maybe he might even guess her secret as Mary had done.

Lynn continued, not even noticing the tear in her eyes. She was completely lost in her memories. "Then I heard someone shouting orders. I turned and saw what was left of the regiment backing up through a clear spot to our old lines. We were retreating. I thought, 'Thank God, at least some of us will make it.' Then I felt a thud in the back of my head and that's the last I remember."

Mary and the officer sat silently, trying to take in everything they had just heard. Lynn was lying still, breathing heavily as she started to calm down. Then, in reaction to Lynn's last words, Mary looked at the pillow behind Lynn's head. Just under her neck was a small spot of dried blood that Mary had not noticed before.

"Darn it," she cried, standing up and reaching for the back of Lynn's head. "You'd think I'd know by now to check over a soldier and look for other wounds."

Lynn let Mary lift up her head and examine the wound. She had completely forgotten that it was there. She did not feel any pain. Whatever it was that struck her had only left a small scar and a little blood. Lynn's real concern was her leg.

"Well, it looks like you were through quite a scrap," the officer said to Lynn as he stood up. "But it also looks like you'll make it," he added as he looked down at Lynn's leg.

Lynn's eyes followed his and she stared at her leg. She lay as motionless as possible, afraid that any move might cause the blanket to fall and reveal her secret.

"He certainly will," Mary quickly added, with an extra emphasis on the word "he." "But if you'll excuse me, sir," she went on in an attempt to get rid of the man, "I really need to finish with him so I can move on to other soldiers."

"Oh, yes, yes," the officer said as he began to back away, "by all means. Goodbye, soldier, and good luck."

"Thank you, sir," Lynn responded as she returned his salute.

Lynn looked at Mary after the officer had walked away.

"Whew," they both sighed.

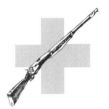

Chapter 14
Brothers and Sisters

"That was close," Lynn offered. She watched the officer move on to other wounded soldiers. "For a minute there I thought he would see under the blanket."

"I know," Mary agreed. "I don't know how you dealt with that fear of being caught for so long."

"You get used to it," Lynn admitted. "In fact, sometimes I even forgot I was different from the others."

"Really?" Mary wondered. The more she heard about Lynn's life, the more fascinated she became with her.

"Yeah," Lynn chuckled. "In fact, one time, when we were eating, I belched louder than an elephant and everyone burst out laughing."

"Oh my!" Mary said, laughing as well. "It must have been fun, being able to be yourself. I mean, to be free to do what you want. Well, not really, of course, you still had to hide, but I mean to be able to do what you felt like doing instead of worrying what people think. I mean..."

"Don't worry," Lynn smiled. "I know what you're trying to say and in a way you're right. I did get to do some things that I had never done before, like smoke and be crude and rude."

"Ha-ha," Mary laughed. "You make boys sound like little pigs."

"Well, they are, aren't they?" Lynn laughed. "Swearing and carrying on like no one is watching them."

"You bet," Mary agreed.

Both girls laughed some more. They realized that they had much more in common than they thought. They both were stuck in a man's world acting as much like a man as they could. If they didn't laugh, they'd probably cry.

The laughter eventually died down and the girls sat quietly. They looked at each other and tried to think of something to say to break the awkward silence.

"Now what?" Mary finally said as her thoughts became more serious. She pulled the blanket off Lynn and began to clean her wound again. "We've got to do something about you. I can't stay here and guard you forever."

"Just let me go," Lynn said simply.

"I can't do that," Mary said defensively. "Your leg still needs to heal. If we don't keep an eye on it, you could lose it."

"I'll be fine," Lynn protested.

"No, you won't!" Mary almost shouted again. Both girls looked around to see if anyone had noticed but no one did. Mary lowered her voice and continued. "I may have agreed to help you keep your secret but there is no way I'm going to help you leave here and lose your leg. That's not why I came here."

"Well, then what are you going to do?" Lynn shot back. "You said yourself that you can't guard me the whole time."

"I-I don't know," Mary answered slowly. "I've got too much work here. If I slow up to help you, someone would notice that I was spending so much time with you and they would start to wonder."

"We need some help," Lynn offered.

"Yeah," Mary agreed. "But who?"

"Daniel!" Lynn shouted. "Of course, my brother Daniel. He'll help."

"But how do we get him?" Mary asked.

"Just go find him," Lynn answered. "He's in the 7th Maine with me, under Major General Smith in the VI Corps."

"I can't go wandering around the camps," Mary protested.

"Why not?" Lynn wondered.

"Because I'm a young, single woman," Mary explained, repeating the words that Clara Barton herself had used. "If I go wandering around an army camp, people will think that I am there trying to find a man."

"Oh," Lynn said. "I get it. But then..."

"Thomas!" Mary shouted. "I'll go get Thomas. He's in the 71st under Sumner. He'll be able to find Daniel and no one will bother me if they know I am looking for my brother!"

Lynn's eyes lit up. Mary's plan sounded good.

"Well, then go get him!" Lynn cried happily.

Mary ran off, stopped, and turned back to Lynn.

"Don't let anyone look at you until I get back," she instructed as she covered Lynn up again. "Your wound is all clean for now, so no one will need to see it for a day or so."

"O.K.," Lynn agreed with a smile. "Now, get out of here," she laughed as she urged Mary on with a wave of her hands. "You've got work to do!"

Mary ran out of the church. She was more excited than she expected to be. She hadn't seen Thomas since before the battle and, she thought shamefully, she hadn't even had time to check up on him and see how he was doing.

My God, she suddenly realized, *what if he was killed?*

Thoughts of her brother's possible death became more powerful as she made her way out of Frederick and towards the army camps around Sharpsburg. There were wounded men everywhere. It was two days after the battle and still the lines of wounded stretched from every church, house, and government building. No one could believe that one day's battle could produce so many thousands of dead and wounded men. Mary began to doubt if her brother could ever have survived in that slaughterhouse.

It took several hours for her to make her way to the army camps. She had to ask one or two different wagons for a ride but once she was there she realized that locating Thomas' unit would be no easy task. There were literally thousands of soldiers in the area. General McClellan was afraid to pursue General Lee and so the entire army was sitting around waiting for orders. Mary couldn't believe that all these men were just being told to wait while General Lee got farther into his home state and safety.

The soldiers were more friendly than she expected. No one treated her like Miss Barton had suggested and indeed they seemed pleased to be able to help a girl locate her brother. Several soldiers even offered to personally escort her to the 71st Pennsylvania. Mary gladly accepted their help. Talking with them kept her mind off wondering about Thomas.

They walked around for almost an hour trying to find the 71st. Because of the thousands of soldiers, supply wagons, medical people, and everyone else it was difficult to find anyone quickly. Eventually, after asking several different officers, they found the camp where Thomas was supposed to be.

"They're over there," the younger soldier said as he pointed towards a group of soldiers camped nearby. "I'm not sure who's in command. We've lost so many officers lately."

"Thanks," Mary said sincerely. "You've been a big help."

"No problem," the other soldier said. "Hope you find your brother."

"Thanks," Mary repeated as she began to walk towards the camp. "And good luck!" she shouted as the soldiers turned and walked in the other direction.

Mary looked at the soldiers in the camp. Some were playing cards, others were playing checkers. Some were writing letters home and others were cleaning their rifles. A few of them were standing around doing nothing. It was a playful atmosphere with laughing and joking and playing and arguing. It amazed Mary how quickly they all forgot the battles and acted as if nothing had happened.

She searched a while longer and began to get nervous again. *What if Thomas had been killed or was in a hospital somewhere?*

The soldiers were scattered throughout the camp. It was a mass of blue uniforms and to Mary they all looked identical. How would she ever find her brother?

Then, in the corner of her eye, she saw a boy throwing a baseball. She smiled and turned towards the boy.

He was a tall, blond soldier, with broad shoulders and a strong throwing arm. She didn't see her brother right away but she knew that he had to be nearby. Thomas loved to play baseball, ever since their older brother David had taught him. If Thomas was anywhere nearby, he'd be throwing the ball as well.

Then, she saw him. He had his back to her and was throwing the ball back to the blond kid. Mary knew it was Thomas right away. She'd recognize that jet black hair and throwing style anywhere. She ran towards him.

"Thomas!" she cried in joy and relief. He was alive and Mary was so excited to see him!

Thomas turned at the sound of his name and looked around to see who called him.

"Mary!" he shouted, "What are you doing here?"

Before he could get an answer, Mary grabbed him and wrapped him in a huge bear hug.

"Thomas!" she cried again. "You're alive, you're alive!"

"Of course I am," he said laughing as he returned her hug.

"I was so worried," Mary began, still holding him firmly. "With all the dead and wounded, I feared the worst."

Thomas hugged her tighter in response. It felt great seeing his sister again. He wanted to tell her so much— how he had fought, how his friends in the regiment had accepted him, and how much he missed her. He had always been able to talk to Mary about anything.

"Oh, I missed you so much," Mary said, returning his tight hug with one of her own.

Thomas hugged Mary one last time and then pushed her back a little so he could look at her.

"Mary," he said with a look of concern, "what are you doing here? Is everything alright?"

"Oh yes, Thomas," Mary replied quickly, holding his hand and squeezing it for reassurance. "Everything is fine. Better than I could have ever expected, at least for me."

"Well, then don't get me wrong," he replied, "but, why are you here?"

"Is there a place we can talk in private?" Mary said mysteriously as she looked around at the other soldiers who had begun to gather around them.

"Yes, sure," Thomas answered, following her eyes and looking at his fellow soldiers. "Follow me."

The two of them headed to a spot away from the camp where they could sit under a tree and talk. Mary spread out some leaves, patted down her dress, and sat down.

"Have a seat," she told her brother.

Thomas sat down and waited for her to begin. He couldn't imagine what Mary had on her mind. She had always managed to surprise him, even when he was a little kid.

"Thomas," she began. She wasn't sure exactly how she would tell him. She was even a little worried that he might not believe her or refuse to help. But she had no choice. He was her only hope. "Remember how important it was to me to find a way to help out in the war effort?..."

She explained the whole thing: her time with Clara Barton, the front lines, the hospital and finally, the girl she found in disguise. Through it all, Thomas sat quietly and listened.

"You want me to do what?" he cried when she was done. He could believe the story about sneaking on the wagon. Mary had always done whatever she wanted. He could even believe she was with Clara Barton. The news of her actions had already begun to spread. But he found it almost impossible to believe that a girl had disguised herself as a soldier and fooled people for so long. Even worse, Mary was trying to get him to help her. Was she crazy?

"It's just for a little while," Mary pleaded. "Until she is well enough to get out of bed. If you and her brother..."

"Brother?" Thomas repeated.

"She has a twin brother," Mary explained. "He helped her conceal that she was a girl."

"A twin brother," Thomas repeated. "This is getting weirder all the time."

"Please, Thomas," Mary continued to beg. "You've got to help out. She's just like me, trying to do something for her country."

"You'd never lie to people and deceive your fellow soldier," Thomas said angrily.

"True," Mary admitted. If there was one thing that they got from their parents it was a strong sense of honesty. "But she's not me. She's a girl in trouble and she needs help."

"She chose to lie," Thomas said. "Let her pay for it."

"Thomas Adams!" Mary shouted. "How can you be so heartless? She was only trying to help! She sacrificed everything, her future, her hopes and dreams, and maybe even her life so that she could help. If anyone should understand that sacrifice it's a fellow soldier like you."

"So what do you want me to do?" Thomas said bitterly. "Become her personal guard? Lie to my superiors like she has lied just to protect her secret?"

"It's not as terrible as that," Mary replied. "All you need to do is visit her, that's all. Talk to her, keep her company and when someone comes to clean her wounds just say that she is fine already. That's not a lie. I'll be taking care of her wound so no one else will need to. You won't be lying and she'll be safe."

"I don't know," Thomas admitted.

"Please, Thomas," Mary begged. "It's important to me."

"Welllll," Thomas said slowly. He had a difficult time saying no to his sister. She had done so much for him when he was little: read to him, walked him to school, protected him from the local bullies. He certainly owed her a lot.

Thomas looked into Mary's eyes. This meant something to her. It was not just a favor she was asking for. For whatever reason, this soldier had touched Mary. She seemed to care about what happened to her. If Thomas said no, Mary might never forgive him. Their relationship would be ruined. What choice did he have?

"O.K.," Thomas finally agreed. "But I can't do it for very long. We might be moving out soon and I've still got my regular duties to perform."

"Just a couple of days," Mary cried cheerfully. "I promise."

Chapter 15
The Bath

"Are you sure we should be doing this?" Thomas asked nervously. It was bad enough that he had been dragged into this whole thing but to be sneaking around town with a wounded girl disguised as a soldier seemed a bit much.

"Why not?" Lynn's brother Daniel responded innocently. Mary and Thomas had found Daniel relatively easily once Thomas had agreed to help. After the way Lynn and Daniel's unit had been destroyed in the battle, Daniel was thrilled to hear the good news that his sister was still alive. He was eager to help.

Once they arrived in Frederick, Daniel and Thomas quickly became friends. It seemed that they had something in common. They each had a headstrong sister who was constantly getting them into trouble. Daniel would tell Thomas about the time his sister fought against some bullies and Thomas would tell of a similar instance when he and the neighborhood kids were going at it. Thomas would complain about how bossy Mary was and then Daniel would launch into a long list of the commands Lynn would give him back home. The two would shortly be on the floor laughing while Mary and Lynn looked on in disgust.

"Is he always such a pain?" Mary would say to Lynn.

"Definitely," Lynn would respond.

Now after more than a day of guarding Lynn, they had decided to treat her special. Mary had suggested that Lynn take this opportunity to do something she had not been able to do for a long time, something that only a girl would want to do and something that she missed. Mary suggested taking a bath.

"What a great idea!" Lynn cried. "I haven't had one in soooo long. I used to love sitting at home in the cabin at the lake, with the window open and the cool air blowing over me as I soaked in the tub."

"I knew you'd like that idea," Mary said with a smile. "It's something no boy would ever think of."

"That's for sure," Lynn said with a laugh.

They had decided to try to find a house in Frederick that they could rent for several hours. With Lynn and Daniel's grandmother dying shortly after they joined the army, the twins had no one to send their money home to and nothing to spend it on. True, army pay was nothing special but they had more than enough to rent a room for a few hours.

"This really is stupid," Thomas repeated. "Why do we have to help her take a bath anyway?"

"Oh, hush up, Thomas," Mary scolded. "You've been complaining since we left the hospital."

"See what I mean?" Thomas said to Daniel. "Always bossing me around."

Daniel laughed and nodded his head in agreement. "Get used to it, Thomas," he chuckled.

By the time they got to the house, Lynn was already tired. The boys had been carrying her on a stretcher through the town and she insisted on sitting up and looking at all the sights. There were still soldiers, wagon trains, and reporters hanging around. It was a crazy, noisy, exciting mess. Now after straining to watch it for a little while, Lynn's back was sore and her energy was low.

"That bath is sounding better and better," she commented.

When they reached the house, they went directly towards the bathroom. Daniel had made sure that no one would be home and had paid the owner in advance. He had made some excuse about the soldier needing privacy. They were all alone.

Once there, Thomas and Daniel took a seat in the outer room while Mary stayed with Lynn and helped her undress.

"Oh, I can't wait to get all these months of dirt and grime off me and sit in a nice warm tub," Lynn said in a dreamy voice.

"We won't be more than an hour," Mary told the boys as she closed the door.

"An hour?" Thomas shouted. "You said it would be quick."

There was no response from behind the door. Thomas looked at Daniel in disgust. Daniel just shrugged his shoulders. What else could they do?

After ten minutes or so, Thomas was ready to climb the walls. He and Daniel had already talked about everything they could think of yesterday. Now, there was nothing to do except stare at the paint on the walls of the room.

"Wish I had brought my cards," Daniel said.

"You play cards?" Thomas asked.

"All the time," Daniel bragged. "We got a real game going in the 7th. I'm already up about two weeks' pay."

"Really?" Thomas exclaimed. "I ain't never played cards yet."

"What do you do with your free time then?" Daniel wondered. He thought that everyone played cards. After all, everyone in his regiment seemed to.

"Play baseball," Thomas answered simply.

"Baseball?" Daniel repeated. "You mean that new game from New York?"

"And Boston," Thomas corrected him.

"I've always wanted to try that," Daniel admitted.

"You have?" Thomas asked eagerly. He reached into his pocket and groped around for something.

"Sure," Daniel said. "Why not?"

"Wanna play now?" Thomas asked as he pulled out the baseball. "I got a ball right here."

"A baseball?" Daniel said in surprise. "Where'd you get that?"

"I've always had it," Thomas admitted. "It's the first ball I hit a homer with."

"A homer?" Daniel repeated.

"Yeah," Thomas explained, "A home run. Y'know when you hit the ball so hard you get to run all the bases."

"Bases?" Daniel repeated again with a confused look on his face.

"You never have played baseball," Thomas said in disbelief, "have you?"

"Back in Maine where I lived there was no one who had heard of it," Daniel admitted. "And when I learned about it in the regiment, most of us were too busy playing cards to give it much attention."

"Well, how about I teach you a thing or two?" Thomas suggested.

"Here?" Daniel wondered. "Now?"

"Not here," Thomas snapped back. "Outside."

"Are you sure we should go out?" Daniel asked.

"They'll be in there for an hour, remember?" Thomas said. "What's the harm? We're not doing anything anyway."

"Well, O.K.," Daniel agreed slowly. "But just for a little while."

"Sure!" Thomas said with a big smile as he turned towards the door. "Let's go."

Thomas hurried out of the house with Daniel following. They both were eager to do something else besides standing watch for the girls for awhile. When they reached the streets they had trouble finding a place to throw the ball. The crowds were everywhere and Thomas knew they needed a clear path.

"How about over there?" Daniel suggested as he pointed across the street.

Thomas looked and saw an area of the street that was less crowded. There must have been a sharp corner nearby because it seemed that people were naturally not walking in that area.

"That'll do," he agreed.

Thomas pitched the ball to Daniel. He caught it one-handed and smiled.

"Throw it back!" Thomas shouted. *Daniel's a natural,* Thomas thought to himself. *This will be fun.*

The two boys threw the ball back and forth for several minutes. Thomas gave Daniel all kinds of variations of throws to try to catch Daniel off guard. He pitched it hard and fast, he threw it slow, he bounced it off the ground, and he even popped it high in the air. Every time, Daniel caught the ball easily and threw it back to Thomas the same way.

"You sure you haven't played this before?" Thomas said with a grin.

"Never," Daniel laughed. "Although Lynn and I have thrown a ball around before."

"Sure," Thomas replied. He had figured that. Every kid played with some kind of ball. But Thomas was certain that Daniel had never hit a ball pitched fast at him before.

"Why don't you try hitting?" Thomas suggested.

"With what?" Daniel wondered as he looked around.

"Here," Thomas cried as he broke a railing off an old fence nearby. "Use this."

"Thomas!" Daniel said with a chuckle. "That was someone's property!"

"It was falling off anyway," Thomas shrugged. "Go ahead and hit."

"Alright," Daniel agreed. "Where should I stand?"

"Over there," Thomas pointed. "So that you don't smash a window."

Daniel stood with both hands on the piece of wood and looked at Thomas. "Ready!" he cried.

Thomas gripped the ball and prepared to pitch. Then he stopped and thought for a moment. Something didn't seem right.

"Wait!" he shouted as he took off his hat and placed it on the ground in front of Daniel. "You need a plate."

"A plate?" Daniel repeated.

"Something for me to throw the ball over," Thomas explained. "There's four of them in a game, but we'll only use this 'cuz of the street."

"O.K.," Daniel said, shrugging his shoulders. "Whatever you say."

Thomas backed up again and prepared to pitch the ball. He decided to take it easy the first time.

"Strike!" Thomas shouted as Daniel swung and missed. "C'mon, that was an easy one!" he cried.

Daniel frowned and turned to get the ball. "Give it to me again!" he shouted as he tossed the ball back.

Thomas pitched another one. "Strike two!" he cried as Daniel swung again. "One more and you're out!"

"Don't worry," Daniel growled as he threw the ball back again. "I won't miss this time."

"Yeah sure," Thomas smiled. "I bet you'll never hit it."

"Ha-ha," Daniel commented, gripping the bat tighter and staring directly at Thomas. "You'll see."

Thomas grinned and thought about his next pitch. He had already pitched two slow ones to Daniel. He wouldn't be expecting a straight fastball this time. It would be fun to strike him out.

"Here it comes!" Thomas shouted.

Daniel eyed the ball and swung as hard as he could.

Crack! The ball went sailing into the air and across the street.

"Yeah!" Daniel cried as he watched Thomas turn and run after the ball.

"Excuse me, excuse me," Thomas called as he darted in between people and ran after the ball. Daniel really did hit a good one, Thomas thought. He'd make a great addition to Thomas' team back at the regiment. Thomas wondered if he could add Daniel to his roster.

"You find it?" Daniel called to Thomas from his spot across the street. He was having a great time and wanted to hit some more.

"I think so," Thomas replied as he eyed the ball lying against a wood block. "It's right over..."

Thomas stopped in his tracks and stared. Someone was going into the house where Lynn and Mary were.

"Daniel!" he shouted as he grabbed the ball and ran towards the house.

Daniel turned and looked as well. "Oh no!" he cried as he dropped the bat and ran to join Thomas. "We've got to stop him."

Thomas ran into the house and into the main room. He looked around. No one was in sight.

"You find him?" Daniel panted as he joined Thomas inside.

"No!" Thomas said frantically, looking all over for a sign of where the person went.

"C'mon!" Daniel called as he dashed towards the bath.

Thomas followed. Daniel's mind was racing as he ran. What if they found Lynn? What if they realized that he had been hiding his sister in the regiment for over a year now? They would throw him out of the army. They would punish him. They might even throw him in jail.

"Hey, hey," Daniel called as he ran into the bedroom and found the stranger near a chest of drawers. "What are you doing here?"

"I live here," the man said simply. He seemed undisturbed by the sudden arrival of two soldiers in his house. He must have gotten used to them after all the chaos of the past week.

"Oh, sorry," Daniel apologized. He looked over at the bathroom. The door was still closed. *Whew,* he thought to himself.

"What are you doing here?" the man snapped at Daniel and Thomas. "You should have been gone by now."

"You gave us an hour," Daniel reminded him. He looked around the room for some kind of clock on the wall. There was none.

"It's been long past that," the man said, taking out his timepiece and looking at it. "You're going to have to give me more money."

"More money!" Daniel shouted louder than he needed to. He realized that if he argued loudly with the man that hopefully Lynn and Mary would hear and get dressed quickly.

"Of course more money," the man said angrily. "What do you expect, that I'd just give my house out for free?"

"It's the least you can do," Thomas shouted. He realized what Daniel was doing and continued to raise his voice as well, "after everything the army has done for you."

"What the army has done for me?" the man repeated. "You mean coming into my town, turning things upside down, confiscating our food and ruining our churches and government buildings?"

"We're doing it for you!" Daniel cried angrily. He didn't have to try to yell now. He really was angry.

"For me?" the man questioned. "I didn't ask you to come here."

"Did you ask the rebel army to come?" Thomas added. He too was angry. It was bad enough that he and his friends were getting slaughtered out in the field but to have this man complain about how his life was being inconvenienced was too much. "Did you complain when they left because we had marched down to stop them? Did you complain when they ended their invasion and went back to Virginia after so many of us had died?"

"They wouldn't be here at all if you boys had just let them alone," the man said simply.

"Let them alone?" Daniel repeated. "Let them alone? Why, it was those rebel traitors who started the whole thing in the first place. If they hadn't gone on and fired at Fort Sumter..."

"Thomas, Daniel," Mary interrupted from across the room. She had finished dressing Lynn and was ready to go. "Larry needs your help."

"Larry?" Thomas repeated. He still was not used to calling Lynn by another name.

"Of course," Daniel replied as he turned from the man. He really wanted to let this guy have it but he was more afraid of getting caught. "We'll be right there."

"You're not getting any more money," Daniel barked angrily at the man before he left. "And if you've got a problem with that, go complain to General McClellan."

The man just frowned and watched. He knew when he was beat.

"C'mon, Larry," Daniel said softly to his sister, "Let's get you home."

Chapter 16
The Visitor

"I'm going to be moving out soon," Thomas broke the silence as he and Daniel sat outside watching the activity in the street. They had been taking turns guarding Lynn for over three hours and they were finally getting a break while she slept.

"When?" Daniel said with a turn of his head. He had been sitting next to Thomas on the curb of the street drawing pictures in the dirt with a stick.

"In the next day or two, I would guess," Thomas informed him. "Orders came down just a little while ago."

"You know where you're going?" Daniel asked. He was sad to see Thomas leave. Even though he only met him the other day, they had already become close. He was looking forward to hitting a home run.

"Not yet," Thomas replied. He too was sad to be leaving. He missed the guys in his regiment but it was also nice hanging around with Daniel and seeing his sister again. He certainly was not looking forward to marching. "But if you're wondering what kind of action we're going to see, don't get excited. We're not going after General Lee."

"That doesn't surprise me," Daniel commented. "If we were going to go after him, we would have done it already. He's long gone by now."

"That's for sure," Thomas agreed.

"Think we'll ever finish him off?" Thomas wondered out loud after a moment's silence.

"I don't know," Daniel shrugged his shoulders. "I hope so. We can't go on killing each other like this."

"I know," Thomas agreed again. "There won't be anyone left."

Daniel gave no response. Both boys sat quietly and continued to stare into the street while they thought of all the comrades they had lost.

"I heard you guys got cut up pretty bad the other day," Thomas commented after a few minutes.

"Yeah," Daniel replied. "Got caught in some kind of ambush or something."

"Us too," Thomas said. "Some kind of crazy attack in the woods."

"Hmm," Daniel added, "we were in a cornfield. But it don't seem to matter none. It seems that every time we fight, our commanders lead us into one firefight after another."

"Yeah," Thomas said, looking up from the ground as he spoke and throwing his drawing stick into the air. "It always seems like we're getting the worse end of the fighting. It's been over a year now and what do we have to show for it? We're sitting here in Maryland while good old Bobby Lee is..."

Thomas' voice trailed off as he noticed a group of men heading towards the church. Daniel turned his head and followed Thomas' gaze.

"Who are they?" he asked.

"I'm not sure," Thomas replied. "Looks like an officer and someone from the medical staff."

"Hey," Daniel shouted as he began to stand up and brush the dirt off his uniform. "I recognize that officer. It's Major Hyde! He's my regimental commander!"

"What's he here for?" Thomas asked as he stood up as well.

"I don't know," Daniel said quickly. He was beginning to get worried. "But we better get inside."

The two boys rushed into the church. Major Hyde and his companion had already entered and were looking around. They had their backs to the boys and were pointing at some of the soldiers lying in their cots and were nodding their heads.

"Let's get over to Lynn," Daniel whispered. "He hasn't seen her yet."

Daniel and Thomas walked slowly and quietly over to Lynn. They did not want to attract any attention.

"Should we wake her up?" Thomas asked once they reached Lynn.

"No," Daniel replied. "The major is less likely to pay attention to her if she is asleep. Where's Mary?"

"I don't know," Thomas answered as he looked around the room. He could see a few nurses and other soldiers visiting, but no sign of Mary. "She told me she had to take care of some things."

"I hope she shows up soon," Daniel whispered. He looked around the room, trying to find Major Hyde again. For a military hospital set up in the middle of a church, it was pretty quiet. No surgeries were scheduled and most of the wounded were asleep. Only a handful of men were moaning or crying. One man was yelling at no one in particular, as if he was still in the middle of a battle. But he was at the other side of the church and Daniel did not pay much attention to him.

"It looks like he's talking to the soldiers," Daniel whispered again as he turned back to Thomas. "He's wandering around the room and stopping every once in a while."

"It looks like that guy he brought with him is checking out the soldiers as well," Thomas added. "He's got to be some kind of nurse or doctor."

"I think you're right," Daniel agreed.

"Ohhh," Lynn groaned, shaking her head back and forth slowly.

"She's waking up!" Thomas warned.

"What's going on?" she mumbled from a half sleep. "Daniel, Thomas?" she called out, leaning up on her elbows and looking around.

"Hi, sis," Daniel whispered. "How are you feeling?"

"Sore," Lynn replied. "My leg feels like it's going numb and I'm achy all over."

"Do you think something's wrong?" Daniel asked quickly. All his attention turned to Lynn and his face turned white.

"I-I don't know," Lynn said slowly. She sensed his concern and it made her feel good. But she didn't want to worry him. "It's probably nothing."

"Maybe I should get a doctor," Daniel suggested. "After all, you've only had Mary looking at that since it happened. And she's not even a real nurse."

"Mary knows more than any nurse," Thomas interrupted. He had been watching the men across the room but now he turned his attention to Lynn and Daniel. "She's been taking care of me and my family since I was little," Thomas went on in an almost angry tone. "And she helped out Clara Barton the other day at the field hospital."

"That doesn't make her a doctor," Daniel argued.

"It doesn't have to," Thomas replied. "She knows what she's doing."

"I'm not saying she doesn't," Daniel said a little softer this time. He did not want to insult Mary or Thomas. If it wasn't for them, Lynn would have been discovered long ago. Of course if Lynn died from her wounds, none of that mattered anyhow. "But Lynn might still need to see someone else."

"And give away her secret?" Thomas quickly added. "Is that what you want?"

"I'm not that bad," Lynn interrupted. She didn't like what she was hearing. "Stop talking this way, you guys. I just need to rest more, that's all."

"Hello there," a voice called from behind them. Thomas and Daniel whirled around to see the medical officer who had come in with Major Hyde.

Oh no! Daniel thought to himself.

"Hi," Lynn quickly replied in as deep a voice as possible.

"What's wrong with you, soldier?" he asked as he approached the bed.

"His leg's been hit," Daniel said quickly. He tried to put his body between Lynn and the man. "But he's fine now. His dressing's been changed just a short while ago."

"It has?" the man said with a confused look on his face. "By who?"

"S-s-some nurse," Daniel sputtered out. He did not want to say it was Mary and bring even more questions.

"Which one?" the man asked. He was nudging Daniel gently, trying to move him enough to get closer to Lynn.

"I-I don't know his name," Daniel answered.

"Would you please move?" the man said politely, although it was clear that he was getting annoyed.

"Sh-he," Daniel quickly corrected himself in a panic, "he really is fine."

"You're from the 7th, aren't you?" the man asked abruptly.

"Y-yes," Daniel answered. "Why?"

"And so is he?" he went on, pointing to Lynn.

"Major Hyde!" the man called as he turned his head to the other part of the church. "Here's another one."

"He really needs his sleep," Daniel suggested quickly. He was running out of ideas. His heart was beginning to pound. His hands were beginning to sweat. Where was Mary?

"I'm sure he does," the man said finally. He was tired of all this arguing. "But Major Hyde has person-ally asked me to look at his men. That includes *all* the soldiers of the 7th Maine," he said as he pushed Daniel out of the way. "Now, please step aside."

"Stop!" Daniel cried as he grabbed the man's arm. "Please!"

"What the?..." The man blurted out as he struggled to get free. He pushed Daniel with his other arm. Lynn backed up as much as she could on her bed. Thomas looked around in confusion, trying to think of some-thing to distract everyone.

"What is going on here?" a loud voice echoed in the church.

Daniel and the nurse stopped abruptly and turned to face Major Hyde.

"You!" he commanded, pointing his finger and looking directly at Daniel. "You're one of the Rhodes twins, aren't you?"

"Y-yes, sir," Daniel answered. He had no idea what to do now. He couldn't run away or try to hide. He could only hope that they wouldn't discover their secret.

"And that's your brother, Larry, right?" Major Hyde asked, looking over Daniel's shoulder.

"Yes, sir," Daniel replied.

"How are you feeling, son?" Major Hyde said to Lynn as he moved Daniel aside with a sweep of his arm.

"Fine, sir," Lynn lied. "They've taken really good care of me here."

"They have, have they?" Major Hyde wondered. "Well, I'm here to make sure of that. You boys went through so much the other day and put up such a valiant effort that I won't have any of you suffering any more if I can help it."

"I'm fine, sir," Lynn repeated with as much confidence as she could muster. "Really."

"Corporal," Major Hyde commanded as he turned his head away from Lynn and nodded to his assistant.

Lynn bit her lip. She didn't know what else to do. Daniel stepped back. He didn't want to be close to Major Hyde when he found out. Thomas stepped back even further. He might get in trouble as well. All three of them waited, dreading what was about to happen, but there was nothing they could do about it.

"Please God," Lynn prayed to herself, "help me somehow."

The corporal sat down on Lynn's cot and began to unwrap her bandages.

"Whoever wrapped you did a fine job," he commented.

No one responded. It was only another moment or two now.

"Thomas!" a voice shouted from across the room. Thomas and Daniel jerked their heads in the direction of the voice. Standing at the entrance to the church, waving frantically, was Mary. Thomas let out a sigh of relief. She was finally here! Now maybe she could take over.

"Wait!" Mary cried as she ran towards the group. "Let me unwrap those bandages!"

"What the?..." the nurse cried as he backed up in surprise. Mary was too late. He had uncovered Lynn's abdomen. "I don't believe it!"

"Believe what, Corporal?" the major shouted. He looked down at the wounds to see what had caused the corporal's reaction.

"He, I mean she," the corporal stuttered, "is a girl!"

"What?" The major shouted in a voice that shook the walls of the church. Soldiers in their beds sat up. The few nurses and doctors in the church looked over. Mary stopped her run and stood in her spot a few feet away. The major stared down at Lynn, then back at Daniel, and down again at Lynn.

"A girl!" he repeated, still shouting. He turned around and shoved his face directly in front of Daniel. "Is this your sister?" he shouted.

Daniel stepped back. "Y-yes, sir," he replied softly, hanging his head.

The major turned back at Lynn. "A girl!" he shouted. "In my regiment?"

Lynn looked down. She was afraid to look the major in the eyes.

"You've been fighting for us for over a year," he said to Lynn, "haven't you?"

"Yes sir," Lynn answered.

"And all this time," he thought out loud, "no one ever noticed that you were a girl?"

"No sir," she said.

"My Lord," he cried in disbelief. "What treachery! What deception! What will the others say when they find out?"

He turned back to Daniel, then looked over at Thomas.

"Who are you?" he barked.

"P-private Thomas Adams," he said nervously.

"You're not in the 7th," the major said.

"No sir," Thomas replied. "I'm just a friend of Daniel's."

Major Hyde looked back at Daniel. "You knowingly deceived us," he sneered. "You pretended that she was your brother and more than likely helped her conceal that fraud."

Daniel did not respond. There was no need.

The major stood silently for several seconds. His chest heaved up and down. His fists rubbed back and forth together. His face scrunched up in anger and frustration. He looked like he would explode any minute.

"Corporal," he commanded, turning to his assistant, "have this man arrested on charges of conspiracy." He pointed at Daniel. He looked at Thomas, kept going, then looked at Lynn. "And you," he bellowed, "are never to put on an army uniform again!"

The major stormed out of the church. Daniel hung his head in shame and Lynn began to cry. It was over.

Chapter 17
Which Way to Go?

"I should have been there," Mary moaned in regret. "Then this never would have happened."

"It would have made no difference," Lynn comforted her. "Major Hyde would have still found out and you would have gotten in trouble as well."

"I still should have been there," Mary repeated.

"You had to take care of those medical supplies," Lynn reminded her. "You can't be two places at once."

"I never even got to say goodbye to Thomas," Mary lamented.

Lynn didn't respond. She was too busy thinking of her own problems. Her leg was well enough to walk on now, with a little help from a crutch. But she had no idea where to go or what to do. It was as if she never existed. Everything she had done for her country, all the battles she had fought in, all the marches, all the work, was forgotten. It was like she had never done anything at all.

Mary looked over at Lynn and saw the grief on her face. *My God,* she realized, *what is she going to do now?*

"At least they aren't going to punish Daniel too much," Lynn spoke up.

"What do you mean?"

"One of my friends in the 7th," (an ex-friend, she thought bitterly. They all acted as if she were dead.), "told me that he's only going to be in prison for thirty days, then they're going to transfer him."

"Transfer him?" Mary repeated. "Why?"

"No one trusts him," Lynn explained. "Major Hyde doesn't want him in the regiment anymore."

"But why transfer him? Shouldn't they just throw him out?"

"Major Hyde doesn't want anyone to find out how he and his men were fooled," Lynn continued. She sighed and curled her lip in disgust as she spoke. "He wants it all hushed up. So he's transferring Daniel to another unit from Maine."

"Which one?"

"The 20th, I think."

Mary took a deep breath and exhaled slowly. "I just can't believe how they are treating him." She sighed. "I can't believe how they are treating you!"

"What did you expect?" Lynn snapped. "That they would say 'My gosh! You're a girl! Way to go!'?"

Mary made a "tsk" sound with her lips. "No!" she puffed. "I just didn't think that they'd ignore everything you did for them."

"All they think I did," Lynn snapped back, "was deceive them."

"Why are you snapping at me?" Mary said. "I didn't do anything wrong."

"You didn't do anything right," Lynn snipped.

"What do you mean?" Mary shouted angrily.

"You just don't understand, do you?" Lynn cried in frustration.

"Understand what?"

"You're not helping the situation," Lynn explained angrily. "You're just making things worse."

"What are you talking about?" Mary shouted.

Lynn let out a big breath of air and began.

"Look," she said. "You're here because you think that women need to do more in the war effort, right?"

"Yeah, of course,"

"Well, the way you are doing it is no help at all."

"Huh?"

"Don't you see?" Lynn almost shouted. "You are doing exactly what men expect you to do. You are being a good little woman, staying in your place and doing everything they tell you."

"No, I'm not," Mary shot back. "I'm doing what I think is right."

"But what you really want is to be treated as an equal," Lynn tried to get her to understand.

"Of course," Mary said simply. "Doesn't everyone?"

"But you're not doing anything about it!" Lynn shouted. "All you're doing is telling men that it is O.K. for them to continue to make all your decisions and boss you around and put you in your place."

"They didn't put me in my place," Mary shouted back. "I chose to do this."

"Because it's the only choice you have!"

"What would you have me do?" Mary continued to shout. She couldn't believe that Lynn was saying this. After all she had done for her and all she had sacrificed to try to help her country. "Dress up like a man, like you did? Pretend to be something I'm not?"

"It's better than being something you don't want to be!"

"I want to be a nurse! I want to help the wounded. I don't want to be a soldier, and I certainly don't want to be a man!"

"Well, neither do I," Lynn replied. She was starting to get confused now. It all seemed so clear to her before. Didn't every woman think the same way? Weren't they all trying to get out of the man's world? How could any woman disagree with what she was doing?

"But you are a man," Mary went on. "At least you were. You belched and were rude and made a pig of yourself and fought and almost died like a man."

"You just don't understand," Lynn tried to defend herself. "I did what I thought was right! I did the only thing I could think of besides sitting at home and waiting for my brother to come back in a casket."

"I do understand," Mary said softly. "Maybe more than you'll ever know. But that doesn't mean I have to be just like you. I can deal with the way men treat us in our own way. I can be proud to be a woman in a man's world without resorting to trying to be like a man. Being equal to men doesn't mean we have to be men. It means they have to let us be the kind of women we want to be."

"But how will they ever accept us if they don't see that we can do everything that they can do?"

"I don't know," Mary conceded. "But I do know that you're going to have to find another way."

"I can't go home," Lynn shook her head. "There's nothing for me there except memories."

"Why don't you come with me?" Mary cried with a sudden energy.

"And be a nurse?" Lynn said doubtfully. "I don't know how to do that."

"No," Mary quickly explained as the idea formed in her head. "I'm not going to be a nurse. With everything I've done, they still won't let me help officially. I'm going to have to go back home once this mess is all cleaned up in Frederick."

"And do what?" Lynn wondered.

"Work with Mrs. Harris of the Philadelphia Ladies Aid Society," Mary replied. "I met her the other day. She is down here as well. She is inspecting the camps and the supplies and making sure all the materials they donated to the men are getting there."

"You want me to live with you in Philadelphia and help package boxes?" Lynn said doubtfully.

"I know it doesn't sound exciting," Mary said quickly. "But it really is important work. You know better than I do how much the soldiers need supplies. With the war going the way it is now, our work will be even more important."

Lynn did not respond. She was thinking. *It certainly would not be as exciting as being a soldier,* she thought, *but it's better than doing nothing. And I won't have to pretend to be somebody else anymore. I'll be able to be me and I'll have Mary as a friend. Maybe I could even find a new way to be somebody special and important.*

"Alright!" Lynn broke the silence. "I'll do it!"

Mary smiled. She would finally have a friend.

Epilogue

Battles

The Battle of Antietam was over, but so many more battles were yet to come. General Robert E. Lee escaped into Virginia where he would continue to fight for several more years. Because he was so unwilling to go after General Lee, the commander of the Union army, General George B. McClellan, was fired by President Abraham Lincoln. Lincoln would continue to battle over who would be the commander of the Union army.

African Americans would now join the battle as well. After Antietam, President Lincoln had issued his famous Emancipation Proclamation. Mary had gotten her wish. The war had become a war to end slavery. Equally as important, the Proclamation also let African Americans fight in the army. Over a hundred thousand would sign up before the war ended. Their battle for equality was just beginning.

Women would also continue their battle for equality throughout the war and beyond. Clara Barton would remain on the front lines, and after the war she would go on to found the American Red Cross. Lynn and Mary would continue their battle to find a place in the war and in male society, and through it all, the battle for the survival of the Unites States of America would continue.

Preview

Look for this scene in book six of the *Young Heroes of History* Series

July 3, 1863
Gettysburg, Pennsylvania

George's leg was asleep. He rubbed it firmly, trying to get the pins and needles to go away. He had been in that same position, crouched down behind a tree, for almost seven hours. It was already afternoon and still they were waiting. *When will the darn battle start?* he wondered.

The day had begun as the previous days—hot and sticky. By afternoon, George was covered with sweat and only the shade of the trees in which they hid provided any relief. He had been in this position since six o'clock in the morning and only the passing by of Generals Lee and Longstreet gave them any reason to stand. Of course they did not cheer for General Lee (they were under strict orders to remain quiet) but when he rode past they all took off their hats and saluted the man they loved and worshiped as a hero.

General Lee had total confidence in them. The Army of Virginia had never lost and never run, and they certainly weren't about to back down now. The Federals had put up one heck of a fight yesterday, but the general was convinced that one mighty charge at the center by Pickett's fresh men would put a hole right through the Yankee lines and they would march on to victory.

Meanwhile, across the wide field, one mile away and just barely out of sight, George's cousin Thomas sat by the stone wall and waited anxiously. He too looked forward to the coming battle. By now, the Union soldiers were starting to feel confident in themselves and their strength. They had repelled the Confederate attacks yesterday and now all they had to do was sit and wait for the enemy to storm their lines.

Unfortunately, the waiting was also beginning to get on Thomas' nerves. He and the other soldiers in the company could tell that something was going on and they felt sure that an attack was coming, but again they were not sure when it would start. Some men slept away the time, others cooked, and still others wrote letters. Except for the occasional whinny of a horse or the shout of an officer, it was eerily silent.

"How are you, Thomas?" said a deep voice from behind him. It was oddly familiar, but something about it was new.

Thomas whirled around to see his cousins Joshua and Ethan standing straight in front of him. They had grown a little bit since he last saw them, especially Ethan. Unfortunately, Thomas could tell by the blank look on their faces that they had already heard about Zachary.

"J-Josh, Ethan!" Thomas stuttered, "I haven't seen you in months. How are you?"

As soon as Thomas asked the question, he knew it was a mistake. A look of pain flashed across their faces and they cast their eyes down.

"Not too well, not too well at all," Joshua replied, looking up again to face Thomas. "You probably don't know this yet but yesterday Zachary was killed."

"Zachary?" Thomas said, trying to fake surprise. He did not want to bother going into the details of last night and it didn't really matter anyway.

"Yeah," Joshua replied, "he was killed during the Rebel attack. I lost sight of him during the battle and I knew that we shouldn't have separated, but when the whole thing was over, he was gone."

"Lord," Thomas muttered as he lowered his head in grief. It was as if he had heard the news for the first time. His chest grew heavy and his eyes swelled as he felt the pain of loss. Perhaps it was the look of pain on his cousins' faces that saddened him and the thought of how much they must be hurting inside. Thomas thought of his older brother David and wondered how he would feel if he had found out he had died.

"It just ticks me off," Joshua said bitterly, "this whole damn war."

Thomas looked up at his older cousin but he did not say anything. His mind raced as he tried to think of how he could fulfill his promise to Zachary.

"We joined up to defend our country and have some fun," he went on, "not to be slaughtered."

"It just keeps going and going," Ethan joined in. "Battle after battle after battle. How much longer till the next one of us goes?"

"I don't know," Thomas replied softly. He knew the question wasn't directed at him but he still felt like he should answer. Suddenly, an idea came to him. "Maybe if we stick together more."

"Maybe," Ethan said softly.

"Yeah," Joshua added as well. "Although who knows? Maybe that will just mean all of us get it at once instead of one at a time."

"At least we'll be together," Thomas threw in as quick as he could. More and more, he realized that this might be his chance to get back together with his cousins.

Joshua looked up at Thomas and stared for the first time. He seemed to be thinking about what Thomas just said.

"You've grown," he said suddenly.

Thomas looked down at his body, then shrugged.

"You're not the pipsqueak we used to pick on," Joshua added.

"You're as big as me," Ethan noticed.

"I guess," Thomas said shyly.

"It must have taken a lot of guts to run away from home and join up like you did," Joshua remembered. It had been almost two years now since Thomas had defied his uncle's wishes and signed up for the war. It had angered Uncle Robert so much that Thomas thought he would disown him. If Mary hadn't written that long letter to him, who knows what would have happened?

"Not really," Thomas admitted, remembering how his uncle and aunt and cousins had treated him. "I wanted to run away for a long time anyway."

"I guess we never did make you feel welcome," Ethan admitted.

"No, not really," Thomas agreed, trying his best to hide all the anger and bitterness he felt about them. He wanted to yell at them for all the things they had done to him. He wanted to make them feel bad about all the teasing and hitting they had inflicted on him. But now was not the time. It was not the place. His older cousins were talking to him and not at him. They were treating him like a person and maybe even as an equal. They finally felt sorry for all the things they had done to him! If he got angry now and yelled at them, they would just get angry right back and he would never get close to them. Thomas took a deep breath and began to smile at his cousins. There would be plenty of time for Thomas to discuss the past later.

Then it began. A shrill scream rang through the air, and fifteen feet away the ground exploded.

Bibliography

Beller, Susan Provost. *Medical Practices in the Civil War.* Cincinnati: F & W Publications, 1992.

Boyer, Paul S.; Clark Clifford E. Jr., et al. *The Enduring Vision: A History of the American People.* Lexington, Mass.: D. C. Heath, 1990.

Catton, Bruce. "Hayfoot, Strawfoot: The Civil War Soldier," *American Heritage.* New York: American Heritage, April 1957.

"The Battle of Antietam," *Cobblestone.* Peterborough, N.H.: Cobblestone Publishing Co., October 1997.

Denney, Robert E. *Civil War Medicine.* New York: Sterling Publishing Co., Inc., 1994.

Hall, Richard. *Patriots in Disguise.* New York: Paragon House, 1993.

Hyde, Major Thomas W. *Report of Maj. Thomas W. Hyde, Seventh Maine Infantry, of the Battle of Antietam Sept. 19, 1862.* Http://www.civilwarhome.com/hyde.htm November 25, 2000.

Irwin, Colonel William H. *Report of Col. William H. Irwin, Forty Ninth Pennsylvania Infantry, commanding Third Brigade, of the battles of Crampton's Pass and Antietam,*

Sept. 22, 1862. Http://www.civilwarhome.com/irwinantietamor.htm November 25, 2000.

Kennebec Maine Historical Society. E-mail correspondence with the author re: Augusta, Maine Civil War History. kennebec_historical@yahoo.com: Kennebec Historical Society, August 4, 2000.

Lash, Gary. *The Battle of Antietam.* Http://www.geocities.com/Athens/Academy/1216/antietam.html May 31, 2000.

McCutcheon, Marc. *Everyday Life in the 1800s.* Cincinnati: Writer's Digest Books, 1993.

McPherson, James M. *Battle Cry of Freedom.* New York: Oxford University Press, 1988.

Moore, Frank. *Women of the War.* Blue and Gray Books, 1997.

National Park Service. *Clara Barton Chronology.* Http://www.nps.gov/clba/chron2.html National Park Service, May 26, 2000.

Oates, Stephen B. *A Woman of Valor: Clara Barton and the Civil War.* New York: The Free Press, 1994.

O'Shea, Richard, and David Greenspan. *American Heritage: Battle Maps of the Civil War.* New York: Smithmark, 1992.

Priest, John Michael. *Before Antietam: The Battle for South Mountain.* Shippensburg, Pa.: White Mane Publishing, Inc., 1992.

Quynn, William R., Editor. *The Diary of Jacob Engelbrecht.* Frederick, Md.: Historical Society of Frederick County, Inc., 1976.

Smith, Carter, Editor. *Behind the Lines.* Brookfield, Conn.: The Millbrook Press, 1993.

Taylor, Frank H. *Philadelphia in the Civil War.* Philadelphia: Published by the City, 1913.

Ward, Geoffrey C. *Queen Barton.* New York: American Heritage, April 1988.

Waskie, Dr. Andy. Philadelphia and Surroundings in 1860's: E-mail correspondence with the author. Grand Army of the Republic Civil War Museum and Library, February 21, 2000.

Wheeler, Richard. *Voices of the Civil War.* New York: Thomas Y. Crowell Company, 1976.